"Will I do?"
Anne asked

Nick had said tonight was important to him, that he wanted to make sure there was no doubt in anyone's mind about them. He had even chosen her dress.

Anne had tried the dress on only once when she'd modeled it for him, and had paid no attention to how it looked. Now she saw that the slender sheath positively clung to her. There was nothing self-respecting about her now, she thought as she waited for his answer.

"Of course," he agreed automatically, even before he'd taken a long moment to observe every detail of her appearance. When he had, she saw the slow spark in his eyes as he smiled. "Very nice," he pronounced. "Lord! You look—"

"Like a rich man's mistress," Anne supplied resentfully.

ELIZABETH BARNES lives with her husband and son near Boston, Massachusetts. She likes to see treasures from the past lovingly restored and was instrumental in helping restore the local nineteenth-century church after it was badly damaged by fire. Vintage cars are a long-standing passion of the whole family.

Books by Elizabeth Barnes

Don't miss any of our special offers. Write to us at the following address for information on our newest releases.

Harlequin Reader Service
901 Fuhrmann Blvd., P.O. Box 1397, Buffalo, NY 14240
Canadian address: P.O. Box 603,
Fort Erie, Ont. L2A 5X3

ELIZABETH BARNES

in spite of themselves

Harlequin Books

TORONTO • NEW YORK • LONDON
AMSTERDAM • PARIS • SYDNEY • HAMBURG
STOCKHOLM • ATHENS • TOKYO • MILAN

Harlequin Presents first edition January 1991
ISBN 0-373-11328-5

Original hardcover edition published in 1990
by Mills & Boon Limited

CHAPTER ONE

'TONIGHT, Annie, you've got to be better than ever before, an absolute vision of beauty and charm!' Joel's pronouncement was no more extravagant than usual, but Anne could hear the barely suppressed excitement in his voice. 'Everything's got to be perfect—your hair, your dress. . .' He paused, critically examining her. 'Damn! I've got to decide what you'll wear.'

He was instantly up from the mound of cushions on the floor, striding across the echoing loft to enter her bedroom, the small space which had been used for storage until Anne had come to live with him. 'What's so important about tonight?' she asked, hurrying after him.

'Everything,' he answered vaguely, contemplating the rack of antique clothes he had found for her in odd little shops in Greenwich Village and SoHo. 'What shall it be?' he mused, beginning to examine each dress in turn. 'Do I try for the obvious or the subtle? What will appeal most to a rich establishment businessman? What shall my Annie be?'

My Annie, Anne repeated to herself, and even after a year those two words still had the power to move her, to fill her being with an indescribable warmth. Until Joel, she had belonged to no one; no one had cared—except her parents, of course, but only until she had been six or seven. Then they had forgotten her in the excitement of discovering a new world for themselves. She'd been left to grow up on her own, in loneliness and isolation. For all those years there had been no one to care, until Joel had come into her life—no, admitted her into *his* life, she corrected with a sense of wonder.

Joel had cared about her from the start, understood her uncertainty and offered her his warmth and the force of his personality. Immediately, in just a week, he had taken command of her life, moved her into his loft and begun to make her over and make her believe in herself. 'There's more to you than meets the eye,' he had announced solemnly. 'Under that awkward child, there's potential. You can be a beautiful woman; *I* can create you! Darling Annie, will you trust me?'

She had, always and absolutely. She'd placed her life in his hands, blossoming under his affection and interest. He'd done so much for her; she owed him a debt of gratitude she could never repay! But she would try, she vowed just before the sound of his voice recalled her to the present.

'Yes, it's going to be the Edwardian wedding dress,' he was saying, thinking out loud as he took it from the rack and held it out for inspection. 'Lord knows, I've been saving it for something like this. . .but is it just a little *too* obvious, I wonder?' The dress was still on its hanger when he held it up to her, cocking his head to one side as he studied the effect.

'Incredibly obvious,' he decided, his clever, mobile features lit by a devilish smile, 'but that's what I want tonight. It's no good to be subtle with a rich establishment businessman. He'll have to be hit on the head before he gets the point, and this dress will do it.'

'Honestly, Joel!' Anne smiled affectionately, long since accustomed to Joel's spells of intense but obscure enthusiasm. 'What rich establishment businessman?'

'The one coming tonight,' he explained absently, dropping the dress on the bed and beginning to experiment with her hair. 'Something simple, virginal. . .very pure,' he mused, gathering up her long, light brown curls, trying them in a knot on the back of her head. 'An Alice band, perhaps, or the silk flowers. . .'

'Joel,' she tried again, a little more firmly, but with no effect.

'Yes, pulled back with the silk flowers. . .' He released her hair. 'What is it, Annie?' he asked, finally connecting with her.

'Please explain about this rich establishment businessman.'

'The richest,' he told her with another devilish smile. 'The richest, the most established you're ever likely to be able to work on for me. It's the answer to our prayers, darling Annie. Thea's finally talked her sainted cousin into coming here, and he's coming tonight!'

'Who? Nicholas Thayer?' Anne asked. 'Are you sure he's real, and not just Thea talking a good game?'

'Oh, Thea talks a good game,' Joel allowed tolerantly, 'but that doesn't make her cousin any less real. Nick Thayer is richer than sin, *and* a collector of some stature. It's about time he had the fun of providing financial backing for the next new and exciting art gallery in SoHo.'

'And he'll be here tonight?' Anne was suddenly optimistic, infected by Joel's excitement. 'You're sure?'

'Dead sure. He promised Thea. You see, he inherited all the family money, which was tough luck for Thea—and for me too, because she'd have given me what I need in a minute. But old Nick occasionally gets a case of the guilts where Thea's concerned, then he rouses himself to do something nice for her.'

'And coming here tonight is to be his latest something nice for Thea?'

'No. Putting up the money for my gallery is to be his latest something nice for Thea,' Joel corrected with the sublime egocentricity of genius. 'He'll do it too, if *you* do as I say. For starters, it's your job to charm him—as he's never been charmed before. And you *can* do it, darling Annie,' he continued, seizing her hands. 'I know you can. I've done such a marvellous job of transforming you that Nick Thayer won't be able to resist you! Lord knows, *I* can't,' he teased, smiling as he dropped a brief kiss on her cheek.

Anne sensed Nicholas Thayer's presence behind her even before he spoke. A couple of minutes earlier, as she had turned to study one of the paintings on display, she had seen him start across the loft towards her. She had judged to a nicety how long it would take a man of his impressive stature and bearing to work his way through the crowd, and now she knew he was standing behind her. Two can play at this game, she thought, motionless during the long count of his silence.

She had a sixth sense about people and their intentions, a sensitivity acquired during the painful years when she had been unloved and unwanted. She'd been a freak then, the badly dressed and awkward girl who didn't belong, who had always been desperately anxious to know what people were thinking of her. Now, thanks to Joel, all that was behind her, and she gladly used her gift to serve him.

She already knew that it wasn't going to be easy to attract the interest of this man. Joel and Thea were convinced that Nicholas Thayer would almost instantly agree to provide the backing for Joel's gallery, but Anne knew better. Nicholas Thayer was going to be difficult. When she'd first seen him, she had known he was a man of reserve and distance, of absolute and firm resolution—not the type to be easily swayed.

In a crowd where men and women alike wore wildly colourful casual clothing, he was an uncompromising study in black and white. His evening clothes were clearly custom tailored, and he wore them with the kind of arrogance which usually passed for good breeding. Anne had marked him as someone from a glittering penthouse on the Upper East Side, someone prepared to amuse himself for the evening on the fringes of SoHo, watching the natives at play. He certainly didn't look to be the easy mark Joel and Thea seemed to think he was!

Even from across the room, she had seen the cool grey gaze which suggested that he was too shrewdly sceptical to be easily charmed. It had sounded easy enough when Joel had told her to charm Nicholas Thayer; after all, charming people had become one of her strongest suits. Joel had been a good teacher, and she did her job well. But charm wouldn't work on this man; she would have to try something different if she hoped to accomplish what Joel wanted.

'You certainly attract attention,' he observed, finally breaking the unacknowledged silence between them. 'Are you merely decorative, or do you serve a useful purpose?'

'Both, I hope.' She held her pose a moment longer, then turned to face him, rejecting charm in favour of the direct approach. 'Which would you prefer, Mr Thayer?'

'The useful purpose, I think.' His brief smile suggested that he understood her at least as well as she understood him. 'I've watched you show around two other potential customers; perhaps you could do the same for me.'

'If you like.' She stepped away from the painting, waiting for him to follow. 'Joel represents a very few of the better young artists working in New York today,' she began, her voice even and composed as she recited the well-rehearsed speech. 'None of them was known six months ago, but today their work is being bought by serious collectors.'

'Yes, I'm aware of that.' He paused to glance at the next canvas. 'Unless I'm mistaken, that's a Debasio, isn't it? A friend of mine acquired one—a kind of jagged cityscape. He's pleased with it, although I think this one is better.'

'So do I,' Anne agreed spontaneously, surprised to find that Nicholas Thayer had a good eye. 'Paul works quickly, and he's growing increasingly confident—you can see it in each new canvas, and this is his latest.'

He was no fool, Anne conceded with grudging admiration as they discussed each canvas, and very different from her first impression. He had a commanding—even overwhelming—physical presence. He was tall, so much taller than her above-average height that she was required to tilt her head to meet his eyes. Fine tailoring had done its best to create a civilised veneer, but there was no disguising his broad shoulders or the vaguely threatening suggestion of hard-muscled strength beneath the clothes he wore. He was attractive, although his features were a shade too sharply edged to be considered handsome. Then, watching him smile at some comment of hers, she was surprised to see his face transformed, his features suddenly not so much sharp as clearly defined. The smile served to soften the harsher lines and angles, giving him a decidedly more approachable, even careless air.

He was younger than she had expected—probably in his early thirties, she guessed, and there were telltale signs to indicate that he wasn't the true establishment type Joel thought he was. His dark hair was too thick and untamed to project a properly stuffy image, and he stood and moved with casual grace, hands frequently deep in his pockets in a negligent attitude which hinted at unorthodoxy.

But not, she decided, the kind of unorthodoxy which would prompt him to invest his money in an art gallery— unless she could find some way to appeal to the other uncharacteristic trait she had detected within him. He had a restlessness—almost a discontent, she thought— which might respond to the novel or diverting approach. She intended to appeal to that.

'What do you suggest?' he asked as soon as they had examined each of the paintings Joel was showing. 'After such a thorough—and remarkably well informed—presentation, I can hardly leave without buying something.'

It was a better opening than she had any right to expect, and she took it gladly. 'None of them,' she answered boldly, 'unless, of course, there's something you'd really like to have.'

'None at all?' He glanced down at her, cool grey eyes shaded with speculation and a hint of amusement. 'That's no way to sell paintings.'

'But I don't want to sell you a painting, Mr Thayer.' Things were going very well, she decided with greater confidence, and now she took the next, crucial step. 'I want to sell you a gallery.'

'That's too ambitious, I'm afraid,' he said with a

dismissive smile, but he didn't turn away. 'I buy the occasional painting, but I'm not in the business.'

'Nor would you be. You wouldn't actually own the gallery, except on paper. All I intend is that you put up the money.'

'*Do* you?' She had finally startled him, but she still hadn't driven him away. Instead, she felt a quick surge of elation as his hand touched her arm, guiding her towards a relatively uncrowded corner of the loft. 'What makes you think there's any chance of that? Have you decided that I'm the type to be a philanthropist or a dedicated patron of the arts?'

'I don't think you're a type at all, Mr Thayer,' she chided gently, at the same time noting how the crowd before them parted, people deferentially stepping back to permit him passage. 'You're obviously accustomed to doing as you please, and Thea says——'

'I see.' He smiled unpleasantly. 'Thea's been trying to spend my money again, has she?'

'I suppose so, although this is the first time I've known her to try it. She seems to think that you feel guilty because you got all the family money——'

'Lord!' She was pleased to see that she had startled him again. 'That was forty years ago, and it didn't happen quite that way. . . No, Thea's wrong, I'm afraid. I don't feel at all guilty about that.'

'I didn't think you would.' Anne gathered her skirts and sat down on the bench in the corner, taking care to leave room for him. 'It's strange, isn't it—the way some people who don't have money think that people who *do* ought to feel guilty about it?'

'I'd never given it much thought.' He stared down at her for a moment, a tall and negligently elegant figure, then took the space she had left for him. 'Do you speak from experience?'

'None at all,' she answered promptly. 'I've never known any really rich people, and I certainly haven't got any money of my own. If it weren't for Joel, I'd starve— or have to get a job.'

His eyes narrowed briefly as he studied her face. 'You live with him, don't you?'

'In a manner of speaking.'

'But you're not just a kept woman,' he stated. 'I know a little about you—perhaps as much as you know about me. According to Thea, you serve as a kind of walking advertisement for Joel Columbo's business.'

'That's how it started. You could say that he created me, and he recreates me each time we go out or have a showing here. It's my job to attract attention—and buyers.'

'You don't just attract; you know your stuff. I'd say he was getting good value for the money, no matter how much he's got invested in you. Of course,' he continued thoughtfully, eyes narrowed again, watching her face, 'your value to him now is nothing compared to what it will be if you can get me to finance his gallery. If you pull that one off, your future should be assured.'

'My future already is,' she said with complete conviction. 'Joel and I are a permanent team, and it's his future I want to assure now.'

'I see.' He smiled, his eyes coolly speculative. 'The kind of permanent team, I assume, that's open and flexible enough to permit an exchange of my money for your sexual favours.'

'Not *that* open and flexible,' she corrected, although his assumption didn't surprise her. She knew that people believed she did other—darker—things for Joel. In his clever world, casual sex was viewed as an acceptable form of currency, and there were plenty of people who believed Joel was using her body, both for himself and as a reward for those who bought the paintings he sold.

But that wasn't Joel's style, which was yet another reason why she loved him so. From the start, he had made it clear that he wasn't going to take advantage of her in that particular way, nor would he let anyone else. Without that assurance, Anne wouldn't even have considered moving in with him, but his actions that first day had still been a relief to her. After he had cleared out the storeroom and found a used bed and bureau for her, he had installed a lock on the door and handed her the key. 'That's for you, Annie. You're to sleep alone,' he had told her firmly. 'Not with me, not with anyone! Part of your magic—part of what makes you so important to me—is that you're so untouched. People can tell, and we're going to keep it that way!'

Now she drew herself up and said coldly to Nicholas Thayer, 'Joel and I are a great deal more moral than that. It's the one thing I wouldn't do for him, and the one thing he'd *never* ask me to do!'

'How touching,' he observed with a brief expression of cynical amusement. 'One might almost believe that the two of you are deeply in love.'

'We are!'

'Then congratulations. I wish you every happiness.' He smiled again—that devastating smile that transformed his features, she noted with pleasure. That smile somehow took the curse off the fact that he was enjoying himself at her expense. Not that she cared, she reminded herself; she *wanted* him to enjoy himself! 'But where does that leave me?' he asked now, still smiling. 'If you're off limits in that particular way, it doesn't seem that I can expect much in return for putting up an undoubtedly large amount of money. To put it quite bluntly, what's in it for me?'

'Diversion, Mr Thayer,' she answered promptly, deciding that she liked him quite well. He was attractive in ways both new and unexpected, and it was actually fun to be matching wits with him. Now, waiting for his reaction, she became almost prim. 'If you put up the money for Joel's gallery, you may extract as much *platonic* amusement as you like from the arrangement.'

'And I'm sure there'll be plenty if you're to be part of the package,' he laughed, his eyes glinting appreciatively. 'You're a bold one, Miss. . .'

'Chapin,' she supplied smoothly, 'but you may call me Anne.'

'Of course. Thea calls you Cool Anne and Ice Princess.

I assumed—another mistake on my part—that she was referring only to your appearance. Have you always been Cool Anne, or is that part of Joel's creation?'

'Entirely Joel's creation.' He really was interested in her, she realised, elated, returning his smile. 'Before he took me in hand, I was hot-tempered and frequently miserable.'

'Why?'

'Because I didn't like myself very well. I never fitted in, and I hated all the things about me that he's made into advantages.'

'What things are those?'

'Nearly everything! People always thought I was odd, because I wasn't very good at small talk.'

'I'd say you were very good indeed, but then I'm a little odd, too,' he interjected with a conspiratorial grin. 'I suppose the point is that the Ice Princess—Cool Anne—doesn't have to bother with what most people think is small talk.'

'That's right! You can't imagine what a relief it is, not to worry about that any more. And I don't have to worry about my appearance either.'

'What was wrong with that?'

'I hated myself! I was too thin——'

'Merely slender,' he objected, 'or did Joel fatten you up a bit?'

'Of course not! He chose my clothes to hide the worst of my defects.'

'He did considerably more than that,' Nicholas Thayer observed, his gaze lingering with impersonal admiration on the soft swell of her breasts, emphasised by the lines of her dress.

'And I was too tall,' she continued, wondering if he would be able to tell she was blushing.

'Not too tall for me.'

'Only because you're so much taller. You wouldn't like me as well if I towered over you. Men never do.'

'So what did Joel do about that? Cut off a few inches?'

'He taught me not to slouch, and the trick of standing

a little away from people, so that they don't have to look up.'

'More of Cool Anne, keeping her distance,' he mused absently, then asked, 'But what do your parents think of all this? Doesn't it bother them that their daughter is living such an unconventional life with an artist of sorts, in a loft in a part of New York that's neither fashionable nor particularly safe?'

'To the extent that they care at all, they're jealous,' Anne explained ruefully, wondering why she was telling Nicholas Thayer quite so much about herself. Now that she had Joel, her parents' lack of interest no longer had the power to hurt her, but she still didn't *tell* people about this part of her life! Of course, she was supposed to keep this man amused, but that still didn't explain why she was talking about her family—except that he had such a way of *listening*, of appearing completely absorbed by her story. 'You see, I'm not really living with Joel,' she confided now, wanting him to understand. 'That is, we're not sleeping together—which is the part my parents *can't* understand.'

'How extraordinary!'

'What? My parents' attitude, or the fact that Joel and I aren't sleeping together?'

'Both, I suppose.'

'Joel and I aren't ready for that, which my parents think is weird. They're ageing hippies who dropped out of society when I was about six. One day, we were living a nice middle-class existence in a comfortable but undoubtedly dull suburb. The next, they'd chucked everything and become flower children. That was in the late sixties, when so many young people were doing it, and my parents joined the movement—sold the house, quit the job, moved to a strange little commune in upstate New York. They're still there—the place keeps going, to my surprise—and it's the sort of place where marriage isn't taken very seriously. My parents have had a number of relationships of various kinds—which is why they can't understand why I'm not sleeping with

Joel. I'm afraid they see it as a criticism of them, and in a way I suppose it is. I just find the whole business. . .well, awkward, I suppose you'd say. It's the uncertainty of it all. I need a little more stability, so I've decided that I won't sleep with a man until I know I'm so much in love with him that I'm sure there will never be anyone else—until there's a commitment of that magnitude.'

'And you and Joel obviously don't have a commitment of that magnitude.'

'No. Not yet, anyway. I wish we did,' she admitted honestly, 'but Joel isn't ready for that sort of thing.'

'I wouldn't have thought you were either. Aren't you far too young to be thinking of marriage?'

'I'm twenty-four, which is certainly old enough, and I'm absolutely sure that Joel is the man for me. It's just a case of being patient and giving him time to get used to the idea, that's all.'

'As easy as that?' he asked sceptically.

'Absolutely.' She hesitated, then took another daring step. 'Of course, it would be easier if this business of the gallery were settled. Joel wants it so badly, you see, and it's always on his mind. He'd have more time to get used to the idea of being married, if he finally had the gallery.'

'Am I expected to play marriage broker?' Nicholas Thayer demanded, laughing all the same. 'You're absolutely shameless—you realise that, don't you?'

'Yes, but what's the harm? If it works, I think it would please all of us. Joel and I would be very happy, and you, I think, might find it entertaining.'

'Find *you* entertaining,' he corrected carelessly, 'but there's a problem. If I agree to this mad scheme too quickly, I'll be left to deal with some dreary business type, won't I? All he'll do is talk about profit and loss statements, agreements and contracts, the amount of capital required. Where's the entertainment value for me in that?' he asked with a smile.

'But I'm the dreary business type you'd be dealing with,' Anne explained, returning his smile. 'I'm the one who knows all those things, who's been out looking at places and figuring what it's all going to cost. You'd be dealing with me, and I'd try to make it as entertaining as possible.'

'Yes, well. . .' He hesitated briefly. 'You've made it almost too good to turn down, haven't you?'

'I hope so,' she agreed demurely, but her heart was racing.

'Still, I haven't said yes,' he warned, 'although I am tempted. Tomorrow—late afternoon—I'll come here for you, and you can take me around to see some of those places you've been looking at.'

'Why?' she dared to ask. 'To see what you think of the places I show you, or to find out if I continue to amuse you?'

'The latter, of course.' He stood up, offering his hand to her. 'There's no sense pretending that there's any logic to this arrangement, but I'm in the mood to be diverted—among other things. I can afford to pay for the service, and I think it's very likely that you can provide what I want.'

Good God! Anne said to herself, suddenly light-headed, grateful when Nicholas Thayer released her hand. If he'd held it any longer he would have felt it trembling, and that might have ruined the effect she'd worked so hard to achieve.

'Honestly, Nick! The two of you have been talking for hours!' Thea bore down on them, a hard edge to her voice. 'I know Anne's the one who handles all the dreary business details,' she pouted, while over her head Nick flashed Anne a quick smile, 'but I think you should have met Joel first. After all, Anne really has nothing to do with the decisions that matter!'

'Calm down, Thea.' Nick caught her hands, turning her away from Anne. 'And don't be such a bitch,' he added in an undertone as Anne backed off, instinctively seeking Joel.

'Annie, are you all right?' Joel asked sharply when she reached him, slipping his arm around her shoulders as he saw her pale face. 'I've been worried to death about you! What took you so long? What were the two of you talking about all that time?'

'The gallery,' she managed, leaning against him, needing the support of his arms as doubts assailed her. 'Joel, I don't know if I pulled it off or not! He wants me to show him the places I've been looking at, but that's only because I amuse him. He——'

'Wait a minute, darling. Take it easy,' he soothed, touching his lips briefly to her cheek. 'You're a bundle of nerves, and we can't discuss this here. Let's go hide in the kitchen, and you can explain things properly.' His arm still around her shoulders, he manoeuvred them into the tiny room, closing the door firmly behind them.

'Now, what's this all about?' he asked, releasing her to search through the debris of the party until he found a little wine in a nearly empty bottle. 'You were supposed to *charm* him, Annie! What the devil is this about amusing him?'

'He wasn't about to be charmed,' she explained defensively, shaking her head when he offered her a glass of wine. 'He's too sharp for that, but he's willing to consider backing you if I amuse him.'

'He said that?'

'Well, it was really my idea, but he seemed to like it. He wants me to show him places and discuss the business aspects, and if I'm amusing enough, he *may* back the gallery. When we were talking about it, it seemed like a grand idea, but I don't know what I was thinking of. It's never going to work, Joel! He's too rational a person to put up so much money for a reason like that. Even if he would, I'll never manage to keep on amusing him. I was mad to even think of it!'

'Well, now that you have, you'd damn well better keep it up,' said Joel sharply, staring down at the wine she had rejected before draining the glass himself. 'Look, Annie,' he continued more reasonably, 'it shouldn't be too hard. Any fool can tell that he was fascinated by you, so you've got him right where I want him. He won't back out now.'

'But I'm afraid he will,' she confessed miserably, hearing the hard edge of angry impatience in Joel's voice. That edge was something new, a tone he'd never used with her before. Not that she blamed him! she assured herself hastily. After all, his future as much as hers was at stake right now; nevertheless, his new mood frightened her. 'Please try to understand,' she appealed. 'He's thinking of putting up the money for all the wrong reasons—and what if I don't keep on amusing him? What then?'

'You've got to, Annie! It shouldn't take much to keep a jaded businessman amused. Thea says he's not a very happy man, so all you've got to do is keep up whatever it was you did tonight. Stop fussing, darling,' he told her, relenting enough to kiss her briefly on the forehead. 'It will all work out—you'll see,' he added over his shoulder as he went back into the loft.

Left alone in the tiny kitchen, Anne felt a dull knot of fear building in the region of her heart. Nick Thayer would discover that she wasn't as amusing as he'd thought, and he wouldn't put up the money for the gallery. Joel would be bitter; he'd blame her for ruining his chances—and then what would happen to all her hopes and plans for the future?

From the other side of the loft, Nick had watched Anne make her way to Joel's side, had watched as Joel dropped a kiss on her cheek just before he led her away. An interesting girl, Nick thought, visualising her in his mind. Remarkably attractive, too, he decided with the detached appreciation of a connoisseur.

Her dress was absurd, of course, an antique creamy confection of satin and lace. Still, it suited her, because she was so delightfully old-fashioned herself. Her features had a grave and composed regularity, brought to life by her slightly slanted deep green eyes. Her long brown hair lent itself well to its simple style: drawn back from her face and caught by a cluster of silk flowers. Yes. . .Anne Chapin was unexpected, but she just might do, he suddenly realised. She might do very well indeed. . .

'Let's go,' he said abruptly, interrupting Thea's empty chatter when he saw Joel appear again, heading straight towards them. 'I've had enough for tonight.'

'But you haven't met Joel,' Thea complained. 'You must talk to Joel!'

'I can do that tomorrow.' Impatiently, Nick steered Thea towards the door. 'I'm coming here in the afternoon, so that Anne can show me some places that might do for a gallery. I can meet Joel then.'

'You're going to back him?' Thea demanded, seizing his arm as they started down the first of five flights of stairs. 'You're going to put up the money?'

'I may. I haven't decided yet. Why does it matter so much to you?'

'Because Joel's got such a talent for finding good work, and he ought to have a proper place to display it. He can't get much business as long as he's in that dreadful loft.'

'True,' Nick agreed, glancing down at his cousin, 'but is this simply one of your artistic good causes, or are you in love with him?'

'Oh, love!' Thea laughed up at him. 'What do we know about love, cousin dear? Joel and I go back years and years, and we've been close any number of times. I expect we will be again—particularly if I pull this off for him.'

'Indeed? Where will that leave Anne Chapin, I wonder.'

'What? The Ice Princess?' Thea laughed again. 'Darling, she's not important to Joel—useful, of course, but it's just a business arrangement between them. Why do you ask? Did she say something to suggest that she thinks she matters to Joel?'

'Nothing at all,' he lied blandly, feeling curiously

bound to protect Anne's confidences. 'It's an assumption I made.'

'Well, you're wrong—for once in your life! Joel finds her boring—much too clinging and dependent and too depressingly naïve—but perhaps she appeals to you. The Ice Princess makes a real change from your usual taste in women, but you might find that intriguing.'

'I might,' he agreed evenly, knowing he had made up his mind. He would use Anne; his scheme was already under way.

CHAPTER TWO

'WILL I do?' asked Anne, emerging from her little bedroom in the dress Joel had selected for her first appointment with Nick Thayer. She stood there, waiting for Joel's opinion, but none was forthcoming.

Of course not, she thought, disappointed when she saw that Thea had arrived and was sitting with Joel on the mound of cushions in the centre of the loft. As usual, they were drinking wine and talking madly, so involved in their conversation that Joel hadn't noticed her. Planning the new gallery, Anne supposed, calling his name again. 'Do I look all right?' she asked.

'Let me see.' Joel finally looked up and gestured, compelling her to parade past him, telling her when to turn or hold a pose. 'Yes, I think so,' he decided, absorbing the soft lines of the dark green crêpe dress, its deep V-neckline outlined with paler green sequins. 'What do you say, Thea?'

'Well. . .' Thea eyed Anne coolly, smiling to herself. 'It's a bit daring, but that's just as well. It's going to take more than her conversational skills to pull this off. Nervous, Annie?' she asked with malicious interest.

'No, she's better now,' said Joel before Anne could speak. 'She was a bundle of nerves last night, poor child. I spent hours trying to calm her down. Do you want some wine, Annie? Something to calm whatever butterflies are still there?'

She shook her head, feeling better now that he had reminded her of last night. Then, after everyone else had left, he had stayed up with her until dawn. He had been all patience and warmth—the old Joel, the one she had known from the start—as he had encouraged her to talk out all her fears and doubts. Remember that! she told herself fiercely, remember all the good times! When

22

Thea is here and you feel left out, remember Joel's love and his warmth! 'I don't dare have any wine,' she explained to Joel. 'I think I'd better be as clear-headed as possible.'

'True,' he agreed carelessly, pouring more for Thea and himself. 'By the way,' he continued, looking up at Anne again, 'you can't stay out late. This is a psychological game we're playing, and I want to keep the advantage. Last night, Nick had as much of you as he wanted——'

'—and tonight he's going to learn that Joel controls you and calls the tune,' Thea finished for him. 'He'll probably want to take you out to dinner, but tell him you can't, dear.'

'All right.' Anne nodded obediently, but Joel and Thea had already forgotten her, back to their quiet conversation. Anne was left feeling like an outsider, waiting for the knock on the door.

When it came, Thea answered while Anne stood frozen in place. 'Nick darling, fancy seeing you two days in a row!' She lifted her face for a brief kiss on the cheek, then drew his arm through hers. 'Now you must meet Joel!' She made the unnecessary introduction with an air of suppressed excitement and a sense of her own importance. This, after all, was the moment she had been waiting for, the chance to emphasise the fact that *she* had brought Nicholas Thayer into Joel's orbit. 'I *do* want the two of you to be friends!'

Still in the background, Anne doubted that they would be: the contrast between them was far too great. Joel was a human dynamo, his wiry frame an expression of his intense and nervous energy, and for all the attention and thought he gave Anne's appearance, he cared nothing for his own. He was the only man she had ever known who always appeared to need a haircut, even when he'd just had one, and his clothes were casual in the extreme. Winter and summer, he wore faded jeans and a T-shirt, with the occasional addition of a wrinkled work-shirt over it. His casual appearance made Nick Thayer seem obsessively neat, Anne decided, eyeing his looming figure which was clad in a dark pinstripe suit, waistcoat, crisp white shirt and discreetly striped tie. He was attractive—particularly when he smiled, she remembered—and she knew he could be charming. Still, she found him intimidating, too cool to be completely human and too emphatically in control of himself and everyone else. How on earth could she manage to amuse a man like that? she wondered again, then started as she realised he was speaking to her.

'I said I like that dress,' he repeated, smiling for her alone, his cool grey eyes lit with approval. 'You have an interesting sense of style.'

'But it's Joel's sense of style,' Thea corrected quickly. 'That's just the point—don't you see? Anne's just an example of Joel's taste. She has none of her own.'

'Which makes her even better for my purposes,' Joel elaborated. 'She always does what I tell her to do, never gives me an argument.' He held out his hand, commanding her to come to him. 'What you see is my creation,' he told Nick proudly. 'Isn't that true, Annie?' he asked her with a smile.

She nodded shyly, returning his smile, embarrassed that Thea had brought up her appearance and grateful for Joel's support.

'And there's another thing,' Thea pointed out with a malicious smile. 'She has absolutely no conversation!'

'No one does when you're around, Thea dear.' Nick Thayer's eyes were suddenly cold. 'One of your faults is that you talk too much.'

'And I suppose you have no faults at all?' Thea asked resentfully.

'I have plenty, as you well know, but talking too much isn't one of them. Coming, Anne?'

'Aren't you going to stay for a while?' Thea demanded. 'Joel wants to tell you about the work he's showing.'

'Anne's already done that, and very well too.' Nick was on his way out of the door, forcing Anne to grab for her coat and run after him. 'We'll be a while,' he called over his shoulder, 'but I'll bring your creation safely home, Joel.'

As though she were a thing, not a person! Anne thought indignantly, hurrying her steps to keep up with him.

Once they had got into the chauffeur-driven limousine double-parked outside the door, Nick stared intently at her for a moment, then spoke. 'He takes all the credit for you,' he observed. 'Doesn't it bother you to be treated like a possession?'

'No.'

'No, I don't suppose it does,' he agreed with a disarming smile, ignoring the resentment in her voice, 'because you're so very young and grateful to him for all you think he's done for you.'

'For all I *know* he's done for me!'

'Yes, I'm sure.' Nick's eyes were suddenly as cold as they'd been when he'd been displeased with Thea, and Anne shivered in reaction. 'Anne, don't be frightened of me,' he said softly, noting her involuntary reaction. 'I'm not angry with you. . .but let's get to the business at hand. Which place shall we see first?'

Two hours later, Anne had revised her opinion of Nicholas Thayer. He was something of a human dynamo himself, with the kind of mind which required and absorbed infinite detail, and an inexhaustible curiosity. Because his survey had been so painstaking, they had visited only one of the sites on her list of marginally possible galleries, and there had been nothing obsessively neat or cool about him as they had prowled the building. He'd become an overwhelming physical presence, ignoring dust and grime to bend and stoop as he inspected wiring, plumbing, heating ducts and load-bearing partitions. At the same time, he had subjected her to an odd variant of the Spanish Inquisition, cross-examining her on the subjects of lease costs, location and the expenses of renovating and running a gallery.

'Well, that's enough for one day,' he announced when he was finally done.

'I should think so!' She watched in amusement while he brushed the dust from his suit and then produced an immaculate white handkerchief to work at the job of cleaning his hands. Predictably, when he was done, he looked as bandbox-neat as before. Still, it pleased her to know that he could be as grubby as a boy. 'I'm exhausted,' she told him to explain her smile. 'I should think you would be too.'

'Hungry, anyway,' he conceded, leading her back to the car. 'I'm ready for dinner, and there's a good little place uptown where it's quiet and we can talk.'

'But I can't go out to dinner with you—not tonight,' she objected, the easy moment between them forgotten when she remembered Joel and Thea's instructions. 'Joel wants me back early.'

'You won't make it,' he said casually enough, but his eyes were cold again, his jaw stubbornly set. 'I'm looking forward to being amused by you this evening, so Joel will have to do without you.'

'But you've got to take me home now.' She glared at him, prepared to be even more stubborn than he. 'If you don't, Joel will be absolutely furious.'

'I doubt it.' The idea seemed to amuse him. 'That's one of the advantages of having a great deal of money and dealing with people who'd like a share of it for themselves. No matter what I do, they tend not to object.'

'Joel will! He wants me back early.'

'He wants the gallery more,' Nick contradicted with a supremely self-confident smile, one hand lightly touching her face but still contriving to force her to look at him. 'My dear, I could keep you out all night, if I wished,' he continued softly, and Anne was relieved when he finally withdrew his hand. 'Your precious Joel wouldn't say a word.'

'He would——' She stopped, biting her lip. 'But I can't, can I?' she enquired bitterly. 'You've got me—got *us* right where you want us to be, and there's not a blessed thing I can do. You can use your money like a club. If I keep fighting, you'll decide that I'm not amusing you.'

'No, you're wrong about that. Remember? I told you not to be afraid of me,' he told her with an engaging grin, all the cold self-confidence gone from his voice. 'I find everything you do—even fighting—amusing, and right now I'd like to be amused. You can begin now,' he commanded, taking her arm in his firm grip as the car stopped in front of the restaurant.

'Do you know why you please me?' he asked, lounging negligently back in his chair after their leisurely meal. 'With you, there are no strings attached. You have no expectations of me that I'm not prepared to meet. You're in love with someone else, so you're not about to fall in love with me. You don't want an intimate relationship—which can lead to all kinds of complications. Best of all, I know your price, or I will before long. It's not as though one thing will lead to another. There will be none of this business of escalating from inconsequential gifts of jewellery, then furs and cars and condos, and then—God forbid!—some kind of permanent relationship or even marriage.'

'Is that what women usually expect of you?'

'Almost invariably.'

'How depressing!'

'I agree, which is why I find you so refreshing. You can't imagine what a relief it is to know we can share an uncomplicated kind of arrangement.'

'Even though you have to pay for it?' asked Anne, risking a quick look. 'Even though there's still money involved?'

'There's always money involved,' he said, his face empty of expression. 'I've long since become accustomed to that. Don't worry, though; I won't hold it against you. You've been remarkably frank, so I'm going into this with no illusions. Besides,' he added almost absently, 'you're good value for the money.'

'Am I?' she asked, watching his long slender fingers as they traced the edges of his knife. 'Why?'

'Because you're bright, and you seem to have an impressive ability to judge my moods and adjust accordingly. During dinner, for example, you managed to carry the conversation without once striking a sour note.'

Reluctantly, she forced herself to look away from the strangely sensual movements of his fingers. 'You don't seem like the type to have moods,' she told him, then met his sceptical gaze and remembered the previous evening, when she had sensed a restlessness, even discontent, in him. 'No, I'm wrong about that,' she corrected, 'but I didn't realise you were *in* a mood during dinner.'

'I was,' he acknowledged briefly, and she looked down in time to see his hand clench, so that his knuckles showed white. Then, recovering quickly, he sat back, and his tone was very different when he asked, 'How did you learn so much about the business of running a gallery?'

'I was working in one when Joel found me,' she explained, accepting his decision to change the subject, 'and since then I've taken a few business courses and talked to anyone who knows anything about galleries.'

'Why? To please Joel?'

'Of course. He's hopeless at the business side of things. He never has any idea how much he owes people, and no idea how much he ought to be charging to make a profit. He's one of those people who can't be bothered with worrying about things like eating or paying the rent.'

'But you are?'

'I'm afraid so. I'd already had to, in the years I lived with my parents.'

'Why?' he asked, grey eyes suddenly watchful. 'Were you the one who had to worry about food and shelter?'

'Not exactly that. Living in a commune, that sort of

thing got taken care of—somehow. It was things like dental bills and how to pay for shoes and clothing. . .' She stopped, thinking about what she'd just said. 'It sounds insane, doesn't it?'

'Bizarre, anyway. It sounds as though *you* were the parent, raising two overgrown children.'

'Not really. It's just that I care more about. . .order, I guess.'

'Stability,' he offered helpfully.

She nodded. 'Sometimes I wish I could change, though. My parents didn't always like it, and neither does Joel—especially when I have to tell him that he simply can't afford something he wants. When you're that artistic and creative, it's hard to be forced to think of sensible things. He gets terribly angry with me sometimes.'

'Why?' asked Nick, watching her closely. 'Because you try to see that the bills get paid? I wouldn't think that was any reason to get angry with you.'

'Well, frustrated by the realities,' she corrected quickly, not liking the implied criticism she had heard in his voice, 'and he's always terribly sorry, once he calms down.'

'As well he should be.'

She bristled. 'You have no right to sit in judgement on Joel! You don't understand him.'

'You're right about that.'

'You don't even know him,' she continued doggedly, ignoring his sarcasm. 'I think it would be better if we didn't discuss Joel. You obviously don't find *him* a very amusing topic of conversation.'

'But I do,' Nick contradicted pleasantly. 'I find all your topics of conversation amusing, or of considerable interest—the subject of Joel perhaps most of all.'

'Well, I won't use Joel to entertain you.'

'He doesn't deserve that much loyalty, you know,' Nick said with surprising gentleness. 'You have done— and are doing—more than he's done for you. He's taken an interest in your appearance, but only because he could use it and you, and he's apparently given you a bit of emotional security, but that's all. In exchange, you've given him your brain and a lot of hard work—and the kind of total loyalty he neither appreciates nor returns. Did it ever occur to you that Joel is one of life's takers, and that he's taking an enormous amount from you?'

'No.' For a long beat, the word hung between them. 'Joel isn't like that—not at all,' she continued at last, 'and you must know a great many unpleasant people even to think that of him.'

'In fact, I know very few pleasant people; they're not as plentiful as you might think.'

'Or perhaps it's that you bring out the worst in even the nicest of people,' she countered quickly, angered, even disappointed, by his cynicism.

'Must we spar?' he asked, a decided edge to his voice, and she saw the muscles knot along the line of his jaw.

'You started it,' she reminded him, 'and yes, I'm afraid we must, so long as you keep criticising Joel.'

'I suppose you're right.' He smiled apologetically. 'We'll leave Joel out of things between us, forget him completely.'

'I can't forget him completely,' Anne objected. 'That's not possible.'

'Then we won't mention his name—how's *that*?'

'Acceptable, just so long as you don't forget why I'm spending time with you.'

'No, I won't forget the gallery,' Nick said with weary patience. 'As I have time, we'll work our way through the places on your list, and then I'll make a decision. Fair enough?'

'Of course,' she agreed with a brilliant smile, contemplating the moment when he would come up with the money, when her future and Joel's would be assured.

'And you were worried about keeping him amused—you idiot child,' Joel teased a week later, after Anne and Nick had spent three more evenings together, following the routine established the first time. 'Feeling a little better about that part of it now?'

'Yes. You were right.'

'I'm always right, Annie. You should remember that.'

'I will,' she promised, then asked anxiously, 'Do you mind that I'm spending so much time with him?'

'No, you silly goose.' Joel shrugged carelessly. 'You may spend all the time in the world with him, so long as you get me the money. Why do you ask?' he queried, studying her expression with a puzzled frown. 'You're looking guilty as sin. Has the old boy been making passes at you?'

'Of course not!'

'I don't know that there's any "of course not" about it,' Joel reflected, complacent again. 'You're an attractive girl, Annie, and he's only human, after all. It's bound to happen sooner or later, and——'

'I don't think so,' she broke in to say, but he ignored her.

'——I could get that much more out of him, if you handle it properly. It's all the same to me, Annie,' he assured her, dropping one of his casual kisses on her cheek. 'All I want is the money, and how you get it is your business—Nick's too, of course.'

'You're joking. . .aren't you?' she asked tentatively, assailed by terrible doubts. 'Surely you'd mind if something like that happened with Nick!'

'Well, I'd hardly be in a position to mind, would I?' Joel asked rhetorically. 'After all, I've asked you to do this for me, and it's your business how you do it. Just remember that I'll be everlastingly grateful to you if you pull it off,' he told her, solemn for a moment before adding with a grin, 'and don't tell me what goes on between the two of you! If I didn't trust you so much— with my *life*, darling Annie,' he said with sudden intensity, gently framing her face with his hands, driving away all her doubts, 'I'd be jealous as hell of that bastard. If I didn't know you so well, I'd be tempted to *kill* him!'

* * *

During the next week, Anne spent four more evenings with Nick, and the routine was always the same. He picked her up at the appointed hour; they would examine one possible gallery, then have dinner and talk. Despite Joel's suspicions to the contrary, Nick never once made a pass at her, never by so much as a word or a gesture suggested that he saw her as anything but an amusing friend.

It wasn't until the beginning of the third week that the unexpected happened, and then it was something neither Anne nor Joel had foreseen. The evening began differently, with Anne running late as she prepared for Nick's arrival.

'I'm sorry, I'm not ready yet,' she told him, blushing as she explained the obvious to him when she heard his knock and opened the door.

'Don't bother to apologise.' He smiled briefly, eyes assessing her. She was wearing an absurdly theatrical robe, bright golden dragons embroidered on a vivid red background. There was a rosy pink tinge to her skin and the deep V of her robe framed the gentle curves of her breasts. She was obviously fresh from the shower, her hair secured in a loose knot at the top of her head, a few tendrils escaping to curl damply around her face.

Not bad, he thought, observing her with cool and detached appreciation, his gaze returning again to the delightful cleft between her breasts. She was hardly Cool Anne now, he noted; there was about her a provocative element he hadn't seen before, and an unexpectedly sensual air. He could use this ability of hers to achieve such charming disarray, he told himself, pleased with the discovery. She was going to serve his purpose very well indeed, far better than he had originally thought. 'Take your time,' he assured her, well pleased with what he was about to buy. 'I'm in no hurry.'

She nodded, self-conscious and afraid to trust her voice. He had looked at her—looked too hard and for too long, she thought as she retreated to her little bedroom. He had never looked at her that way before, never done anything to remind her that he was a man, that she was a woman. The sudden reminder made her uncomfortable, made her remember what Joel had suggested, which was bad enough. Even worse, though, she acknowledged reluctantly, was the fact that Nick had made her feel like an attractive woman, had made her aware of just how attractive *he* was. . . Lord! she was thinking *terrible* thoughts, and she made herself stop while she put on the clothes Joel had chosen for her.

'You look like a schoolgirl—circa World War One,' Nick observed with an impersonal smile when she emerged from the bedroom. 'Is that Joel's idea or yours?'

'There's never any point in asking,' she told him, grateful for his cool reaction and for the fact that he had mentioned Joel. Just hearing Joel's name had steadied her, and her composure was once again intact. 'They're all Joel's ideas.'

'Still the puppet on Joel's string, Anne?'

'I thought we'd agreed not to discuss him,' she countered.

'You're right.' He smiled again, the smile between friends she'd come to know well. 'Besides, there's enough to do this evening, without having an argument.'

'What?'

'You'll see,' he promised, his hand resting lightly on her arm as they started down the five long flights of stairs to the street, 'and I hope you'll be pleased.'

'What do you think of this?' he asked when his car had brought them to the very heart of SoHo, to one of the streets lined with boutiques and galleries and chic cafés. 'Obviously, the right location can contribute to success in a venture like Joel's, but all the places you've shown me seem a fair way off the beaten track.'

'Because we can't afford a good location,' Anne explained, eyeing the vacant store before them, afraid to believe, 'and I'm not going to be greedy with your money.'

'I don't see why not,' Nick said sardonically as he led her to the door and produced a key. 'Everyone else is.'

'I'm *not* everyone else!'

'I know. It's one of the reasons why I wanted to see if I could find something better. What do you think of this place?'

Anne couldn't have asked for more. The location was perfect, in the very centre of SoHo's brisk art trade. She was familiar with other galleries on the street, knew that people who bought from them would also be attracted to the works Joel showed. Inside, the shop was well maintained, with severely simply white walls and a remarkably good parquet floor. Best of all, there was plenty of flexible space—far more than she had ever dared hope they could afford to rent.

Nothing shabby or second-rate about this! she thought, dazzled by the prospect. This was the kind of place a dealer moved to after he was established, not when he was starting out. 'Are you sure?' she demanded, turning impulsively to Nick. 'I mean, this will cost a lot more than absolutely necessary. We could get by with a lot less.'

'Money's not a problem, so long as you think this will do.'

'Of course it will *do*!' she laughed giddily. 'It's an art dealer's heaven, but the business won't be enough—at least not at first—to pay the bills.' The moment she'd said the words, she descended to earth with a resounding crash. 'The rent on this place will be enormous, and it could take years for us to become established enough to pay it. I think we'd better start with something less ambitious.'

'Don't worry about that. We can work it out,' Nick said with such certainty that it took her breath away. 'We'll have dinner first—at my place, this time—and then we'll discuss it.'

His penthouse was a surprise, nothing like the traditional, old-money background she had expected. Instead, it was a stagey period piece—like the clothes Joel chose for her—and just as calculatingly clever.

The foyer reminded her of an ocean liner of the

thirties—severe lines, a black and white marble floor and a curving staircase with balustrade of uncompromising stainless steel. Beyond, the living-room rose a full two storeys, a room of dark and muted splendour, with a complete absence of casual clutter. Couches and chairs were upholstered in black leather, and the floor was a marble mosaic of geometric shapes picked out in black and brown and beige. Three walls were of rich brown panelling, and the fourth was all windows, providing a splendid view of the New York skyline, the scene dominated by the glowing, period spire of the Chrysler Building.

It was a cold room, Anne thought, staring silently around her—technically flawless but without a heart. It told her nothing about Nick, except that he had a great deal of money and excellent taste—or an excellent decorator.

'You don't like it,' he observed, pouring two drinks and handing her one. 'There's disapproval written all over your face.'

'Not really disapproval,' she corrected carefully. 'It's just that it's so. . .so relentlessly Art Deco! It isn't a home, Nick. It's just a lot of money on display.'

'But money's so useful—it bought me your company, didn't it?' he enquired with a cool smile. 'It may well buy me more than that before this evening is over.'

'What do you mean?' She stared warily up at him, suddenly remembering the way he had stared at her earlier. 'What do you want?'

'Not now, Anne,' he objected easily. 'I make it a point never to discuss business until after a meal, but don't look so worried. I'm not about to suggest anything improper.'

She wasn't entirely reassured by that vague promise, but she had no choice but to wait, while Nick exerted himself to distract her. He succeeded remarkably well too, she realised only when they had finished their meal. Back in the living-room, coffee was served, and when the servant had withdrawn, Nick poured himself a brandy before turning to face her.

'You're satisfied that the place we looked at this evening will do?'

'It's ideal,' she assured him, wondering at the way he was suddenly studying her, his eyes hooded, their expression unreadable, 'but it won't do. Joel and I couldn't afford to keep it going.'

'That doesn't matter.' Nick gestured dismissively with one long, capable hand. 'I'm prepared to pay all the expenses for a minimum of five years.'

'That much—for all that time?' Anne demanded, forgetting Nick's strange reserve as she struggled to comprehend what she was hearing. 'You're talking about an enormous sum of money!'

'To you, perhaps,' he pointed out with an empty, meaningless smile, 'but not to me. Can I assume that you're prepared to consider my offer?'

'Only if you tell me what you want in return.'

'I don't *want* anything,' he corrected, 'but I *need* a woman willing to give me a couple of months of her time, a woman willing to pose as my mistress——'

'*Mistress!*' The word echoed harshly in her brain. Dear God, what had she got herself into? she wondered, torn between indignation and an absurd sense of disappointment. Didn't he know her better than that by now? 'It's insane!' she heard herself saying, facing him without flinching, a defiant tilt to her chin. 'I don't see how you could think I'd even consider something like that. Your mistress,' she repeated, her voice rising on a note of pain. 'I won't do it!'

'Anne, you're not listening,' he said forcefully, cutting through her confusion. 'I'm simply asking you to *pose* as my mistress. I want the appearance, *not* the reality!'

'The appearance,' she repeated stupidly, distracted by the dancing clatter of her coffee cup in its saucer. Her hand was trembling, she saw, exerting conscious effort to make it stop. 'Only the appearance?' she asked when she had regained a little poise. 'Why not the reality?'

'Because the illusion, properly done, will be sufficient, and because you're so loyal to Joel that I know you won't consider anything else.'

Thank heavens for that! But still there were too many questions, too many things unknown. 'Why me?'

'Because you won't fall in love with me,' he explained a little more gently, 'and we'll both know precisely what to expect. We can have a straightforward business arrangement, based on the price of a gallery.'

'But——' she began, then paused to sip her coffee, buying time while she ordered her thoughts. 'Perhaps I'm being naïve,' she started again, her self-possession, even a bit of her sense of humour coming back to her now, 'but pretending to be your mistress hardly seems a straightforward business arrangement to me.'

'It does to me, and I'm prepared to be generous enough to make you see it that way too,' stated Nick, leaning with negligent ease against the drinks cabinet, every inch the imperturbable businessman about to conclude a deal he had been working on for some time. Only the slight thread of impatience in his voice suggested that there was more than business at stake for him now. 'All I ask is that you spend a limited amount of time posing as my mistress. Does *that* seem straightforward enough for you?'

'Not really,' she told him, unable to resist a smile. The situation was bizarre—crazier than anything she had been exposed to since she had begun to move among Joel's admittedly strange friends and acquaintances—yet Nick was presenting his scheme as though it made perfect sense. Still, given what was at stake—thinking what it would mean to Joel if she could do this for him— she knew she had to hear Nick out. 'What—exactly— would posing as your mistress mean?'

'It would mean living with me—first here and then at my place on a little island in the Caribbean—for about six weeks. It must appear that we're sleeping together, although we'll actually have separate rooms. You'd have to keep your clothes and make-up—that sort of thing—

in the bedroom we'd supposedly be sharing, but I'd do my best to see that I didn't make things awkward for you, and I'd respect your privacy at all times.'

'You're prepared to pay all that money just to have me around, and my clothes in your room?' she asked sceptically. It sounded so tempting, so *easy*! She could do this for Joel, make his dream come true, she told herself, poised between elation and a vague sense of foreboding. She wanted to agree right here on the spot, then rush straight back to the loft to tell Joel all about it, see his face when she told him what she had accomplished for him. The trouble was that it sounded a little *too* easy, too good to be true. There was bound to be a catch somewhere. There nearly always was. 'Isn't that a pretty steep price for something so simple?'

'There'd be a little more to it than that,' he responded dispassionately. 'In front of others there would have to be a certain amount of physical demonstrativeness.'

There it was, she realised, her heart sinking like a stone. 'Physical demonstrativeness'—he made it sound so bloodlessly businesslike, but there was nothing simple or businesslike about it! Physical demonstrativeness was something to be distrusted, something she didn't want. Even with Joel, she felt no desire for that kind of thing, so what would it be like to touch—and be touched by— this dark and forbidding stranger? He was such a physical presence, with such an aura of power and force only barely restrained. Any degree of physical intimacy between them was something to fear, she told herself with a shiver of wild and tangled emotion. That was the kind of thing she had always avoided and wanted to keep on avoiding—especially with a man like Nick Thayer! Still, she owed it to Joel to at least consider Nick's offer; she couldn't back out just yet. 'That's a loaded phrase,' she observed finally on a questioning note.

'But it needn't be a loaded issue,' Nick countered with an easy, dismissive gesture, still the consummate businessman in control of the situation. 'We'd do no more than what would be necessary to maintain the illusion in public. It wouldn't mean a thing to me, and I can't believe it would mean more to you—not with Joel waiting in the wings.'

'Does *he* know anything about this?' she asked sharply, her thoughts in turmoil, suddenly remembering the time Joel had suggested that he wouldn't object if she and Nick. . .oh, this was awful! She felt lost and alone, adrift on a deep and dangerous sea, afraid to ask and yet needing to know. 'Have you discussed this with Joel?'

'No. This is between you and me, Anne.'

Thank God! So Joel hadn't betrayed her—hadn't sold her to this very high bidder! She expelled a long-held breath in a sigh of relief, then forced herself to concentrate as Nick continued.

'I haven't discussed this—proposition with anyone else, nor will I permit you to do so.'

'Except Joel,' she put in quickly. 'I'd have to discuss it with him before I could agree——'

'No, you can't—that's an absolute.' Nick was watching her closely, his austere expression slightly softened, as though he understood just how much he was asking of her, but his voice was cold and his words clipped and unfeeling. He might understand, Anne thought with a shiver, but that didn't mean he was prepared to show mercy. 'For six weeks or so, Joel must think that you've left him for me.'

'He'd never believe it,' she told Nick, forcing her gaze to meet his. 'He knows how much I love him!'

'Then it will be your job—our job, I suppose—to convince him otherwise.' He paused to swallow the last of his brandy, but over the rim of his glass, his grey eyes impaled her. 'He can't even suspect that this is an illusion.'

'Well, that's clear enough, isn't it?' she asked bitterly, her gaze skittering away from his, afraid of him now. Once she had actually liked Nicholas Thayer, had come to believe that he was a kind and understanding man— but now——! Now she knew what a hard man he was, and the determination to do something to dent his cold shell gave her back some of the courage she'd lost just a moment before. 'I can see why, of course,' she told him with a flare of defiance. 'It would be embarrassing if word got out that you'd hired someone to pass as your mistress. People would think you were losing your touch.'

'There's no need for sarcasm, Anne.' He set down his glass and then moved a couple of paces closer, a dark and threatening figure towering over her. 'This is a serious business.'

'I'm sure it is,' she acknowledged, determined to hold her ground, 'but I don't know *why*. I won't be a party to anything wrong, so you've got to tell me why you want me to do this.'

'Yes, I expected that,' he agreed drily, brooding down at her, 'but what I tell you can't be repeated. I must have your word on that now, or the whole thing is off.'

Here was her chance to get out, she realised, then instantly thought of Joel. His dream was drawing her deeper and deeper into this tangled scheme, leaving her with no choice but to continue—at least until Nick suggested something so outrageously unacceptable that she *had* to get out. And what then? she asked herself, staring down at her coffee-cup, its contents now stone-cold. How would Joel feel if she had to go back and tell him what had nearly been his? How easily would he accept her decision to reject Nick's offer? Joel, Joel, she thought on a note of anguish, you're asking too much of me, more than I think I can do. 'All right, you have my word,' she said steadily, lifting her head to meet Nick's hooded gaze, 'unless you're breaking the law.'

'Nothing like that,' he assured her with a brief, empty smile. 'It's for my brother's sake—to ease his mind or protect his health, to make sure that nothing upsets him.'

'I fail to see why pretending that you have a mistress will ease anyone's mind! Is your sex life really of such importance?'

'It is to Alex,' Nick answered grimly, turning away to prowl the room as he continued. 'His wife has been— shall we say—something less than faithful to him. For reasons past understanding, he continues to be madly in love with her, so he turns a blind eye and pretends that the problem doesn't exist. It's not an ideal situation, but it seems to work except——' he stopped pacing to stare out at the lights of the city '—except when she turns her attention to me. It's been a problem since soon after they were married, something Alex and I have never discussed, but it's been there between us. We've handled it, Alex and I, by staying away from each other.'

Fascinated, Anne waited for the rest of the story, noting that there was no negligent grace in his stance now. Instead, there was a tightly coiled rigidity in the way his shoulders were braced, and one hand was splayed against the glass, as though to hold back the night.

'Alex and Liv spend most of their time in Europe,' Nick resumed, 'while I'm based here in New York. When I do travel, I never visit them. That's worked reasonably well for the last few years, but I'm about to be forced to spend at least two weeks with them, and I've got to do something about the situation—find some way to control it.'

'Then why spend the time with them?' asked Anne, her poise returning with the knowledge that Nick had some natural feeling and lacked—at least on occasion— the ability to hide it. 'Surely it would be simpler to stay away?'

'But Alex has been ill for several months,' Nick explained wearily, clearly speaking aloud something he'd spent a great deal of time thinking about. 'There's something wrong with his back and an ulcer, and a lot of vague complaints the doctors don't seem able to diagnose. It's been suggested that at least some of it is emotional. I expect the situation with Liv has something to do with it.'

'All the more reason to stay clear of them, I should think.'

'It doesn't take any great genius to see *that*,' he said savagely, 'but Alex has taken it into his head to try to heal this breach between us——'

'What?' Anne demanded, bolder now that she'd managed to shake his poise. 'This business between you and his wife?'

'Perhaps, although the problems between us go back further than that.' Nick withdrew his hand from the window to sketch an impatient gesture. 'We haven't gotten along in years; I'm not sure we ever got along very well, and Alex clearly wants to end that. He thinks we can do it by getting together.'

'That's unfortunate,' Anne observed drily, possessed by an unholy desire to provoke Nick even further. 'He's going about it all wrong, isn't he? If his wife's an alley-cat in heat for you, getting together is the worst possible way to make things better!'

Unexpectedly, Nick's patience snapped and he turned on her. 'For God's sake, must you be *clever* about this? It's an impossible situation!'

'Awkward, certainly,' she allowed calmly, ignoring his outburst, secretly pleased to have goaded him even further, 'but don't you think you're over-reacting? I don't understand how he can blame you if his wife is a tramp, and I don't see why you're trying so hard not to break up their marriage. I should think he'd be better off if that happened.'

'Not if it happens because of me,' said Nick, all the anger suddenly gone from his voice, replaced by an infinite weariness. 'I can't have his blood on my hands. He's lived in my shadow for most of his life—unavoidably, perhaps, but it hasn't been easy for him. I don't like to think what it would do to him, if his marriage broke up because of me.'

'So I'm supposed to come along as a kind of chaperon?' Anne asked, serious now. After all, she reminded herself, this really wasn't a game, and Nick's distress was very real. 'To assure your brother that you've got no interest in his wife, and to keep her away from you?'

'That's the general idea,' he agreed grimly, driving his hands deep in his pockets.

'Wouldn't it be simpler just to tell her to clear off, that you don't want any part of her?'

'That wouldn't work.'

'She's the type who doesn't take no for an answer?'

'Something like that,' he acknowledged uncomfortably, then lost his patience. 'Look, do we have to dissect this to death? I need an answer, Anne! Will you do it or not?'

CHAPTER THREE

'I DON'T know.' Anne drew a deep breath, nervously fingering the rim of her cup, a million thoughts circling in her mind. For Joel's sake she should do it, yet the terms Nick had dictated meant that Joel would be hurt. For long weeks, he would think she had betrayed him, and for those same long weeks she would be without him—cut off from the one person she could count on, the one who meant everything to her. Instead, she would be living with this strange and overpowering man, and the idea of spending weeks with Nicholas Thayer frightened her. Tonight she had learned how cold and ruthless he could be. He wouldn't care what happened to her so long as she served his purpose—and a part of serving his purpose, she suddenly remembered with a sinking feeling, would be that physical demonstrativeness he had mentioned so casually.

Oh, what to do? she wondered, wishing that her poise of a few minutes before hadn't fled quite so quickly. 'I don't know,' she said again into the silence between them. 'I'm tempted, because of what it could do for Joel, but how can I be sure that you won't. . .that is, that this won't become more than. . .I mean——'

'That I won't take advantage of the situation—and you,' Nick supplied drily. 'You're going to have to take my word that I won't—that and the fact you'll have the lease to the place we looked at tonight, plus a large bank account in your name. If I do anything unacceptable, you can leave—and with a great deal more than you have now. Isn't that guarantee enough?'

'I suppose it's the best I can hope for.' His proposal sounded safe enough, but there were so many unknowns! So much could happen; so many things could go wrong. . .'What about bedrooms?' she asked awkwardly. 'You said we wouldn't have to share, but won't that seem odd to your brother and his wife?'

'They won't know. We won't see them until we go to St Denis. While we're there, Alex and Liv will stay in the big house that belonged to my grandmother. I built a cottage on the property some years ago, and we'll be there. Servants do talk, so you'll have to keep your things in my room, but that's all.'

'I see.' Anne realised that she was still fingering the rim of her cup, pushed it away and then clasped her hands tightly. 'When do you want my decision?'

'Now.'

'But that's not fair,' she protested, beginning to panic. 'I can't possibly tell you now! I have to think it over. . .I have to ask Joel.'

'You can't. I've already explained that you can't tell Joel about this. It's one decision you'll have to make on your own. Besides,' Nick added with an unpleasant smile, 'there's no point in asking him when you already know that he'll tell you to do it.'

'I *don't* know that!'

'I do,' he said calmly. 'Joel wants my backing, and you want Joel. What better way to get him than to do this for me? Think about it, Anne!' He stood opposite her, his hands deep in his pockets, bending down to look directly at her. 'Think of what this will mean to him— and to you. If you love him as much as you claim to, how can you possibly refuse?'

'I——' She stopped, imagining how Joel would feel if he learned that she had let this chance slip away. Nick was their first real hope for backing; there were no other likely prospects on the horizon. More than that, he had made the whole thing seem so reasonable, so simple and risk-free. 'I can't refuse, can I?'

'Then it's settled!' He straightened up, but not before she had seen his brief expression of satisfaction, even triumph. 'You'll stay here tonight, and in the morning——'

'*No!* Surely I don't have to do anything yet,' she protested, panicking because things were suddenly happening much too quickly. 'You don't need me until you see your brother.'

'Sorry, Anne, but the arrangement starts now. We've got to establish ourselves, and Alex and Liv must hear that you're living with me before we all meet on St Denis. Besides,' he added with a cool smile, 'we need a little time to perfect our act.'

'What act?'

'The physical demonstrativeness I mentioned. I can just imagine your reaction if the first time that happens is in front of my family.'

'Oh, God!' Warily, she looked up at him, her eyes huge in her pale face, trying to imagine what it would be like to be held by this tall dark man, to feel his lips against hers, and his hands—— No! She couldn't think about that now, she decided, pushing the thoughts quickly aside as she felt a wave of colour break over her. 'I wish,' she began, her voice a little unsteady, 'I wish that wasn't a part of the bargain.'

'I can tell,' he acknowledged, watching her blush, 'but don't worry, Anne. It will only be in front of other people, and I won't let it get out of hand.'

'You're sure?'

'Very sure. You have my word.'

'All right,' she told him reluctantly, because she really had no choice, and because he sounded *so* sure that he'd managed to make her believe she could trust him.

'Good. You'll spend the night here, which ought to go a long way towards convincing Joel that there's a considerable passion between us.'

'I can't even call him?' Anne already knew the answer to that question, but she needed to ask it. She'd do anything now for some contact with Joel; she wanted it so badly that she could feel tears threatening.

'Of course you can't call him! Starting now, you belong to me. That's all Joel can know until you go back to him—lease and bankbook in hand. Given those two items, I think you can safely assume that he'll welcome you with open arms.'

'God, you're a cold one!' Tears forgotten, she stormed at him, finding comfort and strength in anger. 'You must have been planning this since that first evening you came to the loft. What was it? Did you see me and decide that I was just the silly, gullible fool to force into this stunt with you?'

'It was something like that,' Nick agreed coolly, but his face had gone pale beneath his tan and the telltale muscle was knotted along his jaw. 'I should remind you, however, that I didn't force you to agree to this arrangement.'

'Not quite,' she allowed bitterly, 'but only because you were clever enough to offer what I can't refuse.' She closed her eyes against a sudden wave of weary helplessness. 'If I must stay here tonight,' she continued when she could speak again, 'will you show me where I'm to sleep? I'm tired, and I'd like to be alone.'

'Of course.' Without another word, he led her through the foyer and up the curving staircase. 'This is my bedroom—where you'll be sleeping. I'll be across the hall.' After he had switched on the lights for her, he paused in the doorway. 'You'd better get a good sleep,' he advised with a meaningless smile. 'The first real test comes in the morning, when I take you back to Joel's place and you tell him our news.'

'And you think he'll believe it?' she challenged, staring resentfully up at him.

'You'll *make* him believe it,' he said softly, but there was an implied threat in his words. 'You're a clever girl; you'll find some way to do it—if you really want me to back his gallery. Goodnight, Anne,' he finished abruptly, leaving her alone in his bedroom, as opulent and completely impersonal as the rest of Nicholas Thayer's penthouse.

'Annie! Where the hell have you been?' It looked as though Joel had been up all night. His clothes were more wrinkled than usual and he badly needed a shave. 'I've been half out of my——' He stopped abruptly when he saw that she wasn't alone, saw Nick's looming figure behind her. 'What's this all about?' he demanded, his eyes shifting warily from one to the other. 'What's going on?'

'Isn't that obvious?' Nick asked smoothly, dropping his hand to Anne's shoulder, and only she could know the force of his grip. 'Tell him, Anne.' His tone was light and affectionate, even teasing, but Anne heard both a threat and a dare. 'Tell him,' he repeated softly.

'I. . .' She swallowed convulsively, wondering how she could put it to Joel. He was going to believe—for more weeks than she cared to count—that she had betrayed him. He would think he'd lost her and his dream in one blow. It wasn't fair, her mind screamed, wasn't fair that Nick could make her do this—wasn't fair, for that matter, that Joel should look so—so *diminished* in Nick's presence! Compared to Joel's rumpled state, Nick was an imposing figure. Taller and stronger, he had all the power, the power to crush Joel and make her dance to his own tune for as long as he pleased. Only when he was finally done using her could she come back to Joel and try to undo the damage she had to do now. 'I—I'm not sure how to explain it,' she tried again, her voice trembling slightly. 'I'm not really sure that it makes much sense, but Nick and I—that is——'

'You don't need to spell it out, Annie,' said Joel, a hint of his usual poise returning. 'I suppose it's as much of a surprise to you as it is to me, but you spent the night with him, didn't you?'

'Yes, but that's not all.' She took a deep breath and hurried on before her nerve could desert her again. 'He wants me, and that's what I want too.'

'I'll just bet it is!' Joel smiled, a tight, meaningless rearrangement of the facial muscles. 'I knew you were a clever girl, but I didn't realise just *how* clever. You know a greener pasture when you see one—don't you, Cool Anne?'

No! How could he even *think* that? Anne wondered. He'd known her so long and so well—surely he knew her better than that! The fact that he obviously didn't filled her with the terrible pain of betrayal. But that was just the point! she suddenly realised. Her sense of betrayal right now was nothing compared to what Joel was feeling. Given his pain, how could she blame him for the things he was saying? 'That's not why,' she tried to explain, torn between wanting Joel to see the truth and the need to keep her promise to Nick. 'I *want* to be with Nick. I can't help it, Joel.' There was an unspoken plea in her voice, but she didn't think he heard it. 'I just have to be with him.'

'Just have to get your hands on as much of his money as possible—I'd say that was a little more like it.' He turned on her, suddenly savage, and she involuntarily moved closer to Nick's protective presence. 'You were supposed to get the money for *me*, you mercenary little bitch!'

'Get your things, Anne,' Nick said quietly, turning as though to use his body to shield her from Joel's words. 'Don't bother with your clothing. Just take what matters to you, what we can't replace.'

She nodded, past words, and fled into her little room, shutting the door quietly behind her. It was worse than her wildest imaginings, she thought, sitting down on the edge of the bed when her legs threatened to give out on her. *Why* hadn't she realised how angry Joel would be, how hurt? And how could she blame him? If he'd come home to announce that he was moving in with Thea, wouldn't she have been just as angry? This was what came of loving someone as much as she loved Joel—and he loved her. Love conferred the power to hurt, to wound. . .oh, it was awful!

She clasped her hands tightly, staring around her little room, memorising its details—the clothes rack which occupied one entire wall, the badly scarred oak dresser with its cracked mirror, the narrow bed, covered by a patchwork quilt, the bookshelves under the window with her collection of used paperbacks, the one small painting Joel had given her. . .

Joel! she thought despairingly, wondering how she would survive without him. She *needed* him; it was as simple as that! She needed his steady reassurance, his *presence*, and she was suddenly terrified that if she left now she would never have his presence again. She had hurt him so badly that she wasn't sure she could ever undo the damage she had just caused. When this bizarre business with Nick was over and she tried to come back, Joel would send her away—she'd be alone again.

No! She wouldn't let that happen, she vowed. She was fighting for Joel's dream, working to give him what he wanted most. He couldn't know that now, but he would when she returned with the bankbook and the lease. He would understand when she explained everything; they'd be together again and this part would seem like a bad dream.

She looked around one last time and then stood up, deciding that she wouldn't take anything. One way to keep faith with Joel was to leave behind all the little things that mattered to her—the painting and the few pieces of costume jewellery he had given her. Leaving them behind would be her promise to return, her guarantee that Joel would *let* her return.

She would leave everything except. . . She opened the bottom drawer of the dresser and removed the sketchbook hidden there. Joel didn't like her drawings, didn't like her wasting her time on them, so they had become her secret retreat, reserved for the privacy of her bedroom. Now she slipped the sketchbook into her bag, knowing that she would need the solace of her sketching in the weeks to come.

'I'm ready,' she announced as she left the room behind, and both men swung around to look at her.

'That was quick, and it doesn't look as though you took anything,' Joel observed with a sneer. 'Why should you? You'll be living with a rich man who can afford to buy you whatever you want.

'You'll be generous with her, I expect,' he continued to Nick, 'very generous with my Ice Princess—now that she's melted in your arms. Your money bought you a virgin, and I'm sure you're prepared to pay well for something that rare.

'You'd better get what you can in a hurry,' he told Anne, savaging her again. 'The novelty won't last, you know. After last night—if last night really *was* the first time—you're not a virgin any more. You're damaged goods now, you little tramp! You're the worst kind of whore——'

God, please make him stop! she thought, desperately trying to shut out those terrible words tearing through her like a knife. *Please* make him stop, she repeated silently, then flinched when, without warning, Nick's fist connected with Joel's jaw. This *can't* be happening, she told herself as she watched Joel buckle at the knees. It's a bad dream, a nightmare. I'm asleep. It's not real! From a great distance, she registered the sickening sound as Joel hit the floor, then felt Nick's hand on her arm, forcing her towards the door.

'Damn you!' At last, as they reached the landing, she found her voice and whirled on him. 'Did you have to do *that*?'

'Yes!' His face was livid, a pulse beating furiously at his temple, but after that first sharp word, his voice was as calmly dispassionate as ever. 'I'm afraid I did. There are a few things I won't permit.'

As though nothing had happened, he took her shopping, but in the smart boutiques she fought him every way she could. She objected to everything he chose for her, being deliberately contrary and employing as many barbed comments as she could without provoking him to overt anger. She could not forgive him for hitting Joel or for the unreasonableness of his conditions, and she spent the day making him pay for his transgressions.

In spite of her best efforts, she won no battles. In the end, Nick acquired precisely what he wanted—dresses and coats, shoes and bags, even silk stockings, frothy scraps of lingerie and incredibily revealing lace and satin négligés. Anne hated them all. When she tried them on, she stared stormily back at her reflection, ignoring both the approving murmurs of sales clerks and the admiring light in Nick's eyes when she was forced to model for him. These weren't clothes chosen by Joel; she didn't care that she could look attractive in something other than quaint antique styles. In fact, she decided, the fact that she *did* look attractive in these clothes was something else to hold against Nicholas Thayer: by implication, he was criticising Joel's taste!

'I hope you're satisfied,' she said bitterly when they were alone in the private elevator, going up to his penthouse.

'Not entirely,' Nick answered grimly, his hand closing around her wrist in an unbreakable grip, holding her close to his side as his servant admitted them. 'Parker, we'll be upstairs, and we don't want to be disturbed— isn't that right, my love?' he added to Anne, his lazily suggestive smile in marked contrast to the pressure on her wrist as he compelled her to follow him up the staircase.

He didn't pause until they reached his bedroom. Then, closing the door firmly behind them, he released her wrist, only to catch her shoulders, forcing her to face him. 'This won't do, Anne,' he told her, his cold, controlled anger reflected in his eyes. 'I'm not paying you to fight me every step of the way.'

'After what you've done, what do you expect?'

'Your co-operation!'

'You should have thought of that before you set up those impossible conditions!'

'Sorry, Anne, but that won't do. If you found the conditions unacceptable, you had only to say so. You're not being forced to do this job,' he told her, his grip biting into her shoulders when she tried to pull away from him. 'You were free to walk out as soon as you heard what I expected of you. Since you didn't, you *will* co-operate, be pleasant about it, and give every appearance of being madly in love with me. I won't accept anything less.'

'Well, *I* won't accept what you've done,' she stormed, refusing to give an inch. 'You've done everything you can to be cruel! You don't like Joel—that was clear from the start—and you made those conditions *and* hit him because you'd found a way to get back at him. You're disgusting!'

'And you, my dear, are behaving like a child! Use your head, for heaven's sake!' He shook her slightly. 'I can't *afford* to let you tell Joel because he and Thea are entirely too close, and even you must realise what a bitch she is. She'd love to get back at me for past real and imagined slights. If she had a clue that ours was a business arrangement, she'd make sure that the world—and my brother—knew it.'

It sounded plausible—much as Anne hated to admit it, even to herself. 'That's still no reason to hit Joel,' she objected, refusing to forgive him for that. 'You didn't need to do *that*!'

'He insulted you! He could have said anything he pleased to me and I'd have let him, but I was damned if I was going to let him get away with what he was saying to you.'

'He was feeling hurt and betrayed! *I* didn't care,' she raged, trying to push back the memory of how she'd wanted something—someone?—to make Joel stop saying those terrible things. Perhaps she *had* wanted Nick to make Joel stop, but not *that* way—not with his fist! 'You're so noble, aren't you?' she demanded with venom.

'In character, at any rate.' Nick surprised her with a disarming smile. 'If I really were madly in love with you—so madly in love that I wanted you to live with me—do you think I'd have stood there while he said those things?'

'I don't know,' she snapped, feeling cornered. 'There's no telling how your mind works!'

'Then let me explain. If I'd let him get away with it, he'd have wondered why, and if he discussed it with Thea she'd have wondered too. I *couldn't* let him say those things, and I'm human enough to have *wanted* to hit him just then.'

'There!' Anne seized on his last few words, desperate for some way to rekindle her anger. 'You see? You were just looking for a way to get back at him!'

'For the Lord's sake, don't start *that* again!' Abruptly, Nick released her, shoving his hands deep into his pockets as he began to prowl the room. 'Look, Anne, you've got a decision to make,' he began again, stopping a few feet away from her, regarding her warily. 'It's one I thought you'd already made, but it seems I was wrong. If you like, you can walk out right now and we'll forget all about this agreement. Or you can stay, in which case I'll expect your co-operation and at least that degree of friendship we had before we started this.'

'Friendship!' she repeated distastefully. 'You call that friendship? All you were doing was dangling the carrot in front of me, making sure that I wanted it badly enough. When you knew that I did, you started using the stick!'

He shrugged negligently. 'When you said you wanted the carrot, I assumed you understood that there'd be a certain amount of work in return. If you'd begin to co-operate, there wouldn't be any stick. If you won't, the agreement is off. Which is it going to be, Anne?'

'I don't know.' She turned away, looking uneasily around the luxurious bedroom, its coldness reinforced by the view of the impersonal lights of the city beyond the wall of windows. 'I didn't think it would be like this. . .so hard!'

'Surely you realised that I expected something substantial in exchange for what I offered? You're the one who said I was being incredibly generous.'

'But I didn't know I'd have to hurt Joel,' she said

unhappily, thinking of him now, and of the vast distance between them. She was so alone, she realised with a shiver, going to stand by the windows, staring out into the night with unseeing eyes. She was as alone as she had been before Joel had found her, and the pain of it was almost more than she could bear. 'I didn't know you'd make it so hard for him. . .and for me.'

'But think of the rewards,' he suggested, and she saw his cynical smile reflected in the window. 'Only a few weeks' work, and you and Joel will have what you want—even more than you hoped for. Think of *that*!'

'Yes, I am, but you've made it so hard. . .' She stopped to concentrate on Joel and the gallery and their future together. 'All right, I'll stay,' she announced bravely, knowing her decision had been a foregone conclusion. 'I'll do it. I'll be gracious—at least in front of other people—and I'll do whatever you want me to do.'

'Good.' Nick's reflected image straightened; she saw the quick flare of triumph in his eyes. 'We'll start now,' he told her, coming to stand directly behind her, withdrawing his hands from his pockets to place them on her shoulders.

'What are you doing?' she demanded, instantly tensing as she felt herself compelled back against him.

'Making sure you understand what kind of thing I expect,' he explained, his gaze holding hers in the window. 'I told you there'd be a certain amount of this.'

'But not here! You said we'd only do this in public.'

'Better in private, this first time, than downstairs where Parker can walk in and see how unwilling you are. We've got to touch, Anne,' he reminded her, his hands like steel on her shoulders, forcing her body into contact with the hard line of his, 'and we've got to kiss—at least on occasion.'

'I don't think I can,' she confessed, rising panic forcing her to admit things she never would have said if she hadn't been trapped against him. 'I'm not very good at this kind of thing. . .I haven't done very much. . .I don't like it!'

'You don't need to like it; you just need to do it,' he said lightly, his breath stirring her hair. 'Relax, Anne.'

'I'll try,' she whispered, terrified by his closeness and by the gentle pressure of his fingers as they began to knead at the tense muscles along her shoulders. It meant nothing, she reminded herself, closing her eyes against the reflected image of her small frame held close to his larger one. This was just part of a business arrangement—the money for Joel's gallery.

'What is it—love?' asked Nick with sarcastic emphasis. 'Does it help if you don't have to see what's happening?'

'It helps to think about the money.'

'It usually does,' he agreed with detached amusement, continuing his clever work until the unnatural stiffness began to leave her body. 'That's right,' he told her, sensing the change, 'just lean against me.'

Anne couldn't help herself, she realised, feeling dazed. A kind of mindless lassitude was stealing over her, sapping her strength and robbing her of the will to resist. It was all so new—*too* new! she thought as Nick slipped his arms around her, crossing them just beneath her breasts, drawing her even closer. Now all her weight was resting on him, her body moulded into the stronger line of his, and when he touched his lips to a sensitive spot behind her ear her involuntary indrawn breath disturbed the intimate silence between them.

'Very good, love,' he murmured, turning her to face him. 'Now I'll kiss you.'

Something happened to her in the instant his lips first touched hers; she found herself overwhelmed by the heat of his body against hers, completely absorbed by his clever, teasing kiss. This was nothing like the tentative explorations she had been forced to endure in the past, she realised vaguely, nothing like Joel's brief gestures of affection. Nick was too clever for her, coaxing her answering response as the world swung alarmingly and she instinctively gripped his shoulders to steady herself. What was happening to her? she wondered wildly, her lips parting under the gentle pressure of his, her thoughts beginning to scatter. . .

'Very good, love,' he said again, finally ending their kiss, his eyes lit with amusement when she stared up at him in confusion. 'You respond very well, and I'm going to remember that. The next time you turn surly and dig in your heels, I'll just kiss you into submission.'

'No! You can't,' she protested, suddenly appalled by what she had permitted—possibly even wanted—to happen between them. 'I won't let you!'

'You won't have any choice, love. This may be new to you, but you like it.' He caught her to him again, bending his head so that his lips could again tease at hers. 'Don't you like this, Cool Anne?'

'No!' Don't let him do this, she urged herself, trying to fight the weakness already invading her limbs. 'Please don't,' she whispered, turning her head to avoid his kiss, placing her palms flat against his chest in an ineffectual attempt to push him away.

'Anne, I'm paying you for this,' he reminded her, drawing her closer, his lips touching her temple, then tracing the curve of her cheek. 'Let me kiss you.'

She tried to protest, but he stopped her, taking advantage of her parted lips to kiss her with invasive deliberation, and instantly she was lost. Wanting this. . .wanting him, she thought distractedly, suddenly knowing how the moth feels when drawn to the flame. She was helpless, beyond any will to fight him, and it wasn't until he chose to end the kiss that she finally managed to draw together the scattered remnants of her resistance. 'Damn you,' she said unsteadily. 'That was unfair.'

'Unexpected,' he corrected absently, his eyes a dark and smouldering grey. 'There's a certain amount of chemistry between us, you know,' he explained with a lazy smile, still holding her so close that she was sure he could feel the wild pounding of her heart. 'Why don't you try to relax and enjoy it as much as I intend to?'

'You'd like that, wouldn't you?'

'I *will* like it,' he promised, still smiling. 'There's going to be nothing tedious about this arrangement. . .I'm very pleased, Cool Anne. You're more of a bargain than I expected, and I won't forget that when it's time to settle up. And don't look quite so stricken, love,' he added softly, watching her expression. 'This doesn't *mean* anything, but it's amusing, and it should go a long way towards creating the illusion I want.'

Abruptly he released her and left the room, leaving her feeling dazed. 'Dear God,' she whispered, lowering herself to the edge of the bed when her legs threatened to give out on her. What had *possessed* her? To respond to Nicholas Thayer as she had never thought of responding to Joel was an obscenity, one that filled her with shame and self-loathing. What she had done was a violation both of herself and of her love for Joel!

Joel's style—and hers too! she reminded herself—was the brief kiss and the casual embrace, those cool and careful gestures of affection which made no demands. There had been a few times when Joel had held her close, but those had all been in the early days of their relationship when she had still felt lost and lonely and unsure of herself. Joel hadn't held her that way—there'd been no need for him to hold her that way!—for months. And she had never, never, *never* felt with Joel as she had with Nicholas Thayer. . .

She didn't *want* to feel that way! She hated mindless physical need, those emotions which had created such chaos in her parents' lives and hers. There was nothing safe, nothing *sure*, about passion! It complicated everything, corrupted and destroyed the love between two people; she had watched it happen to her parents, had watched passion rule their lives until there had been nothing left of the family she had once had. At first, of course, she hadn't understood. As a child, she hadn't been able to make sense of the constantly changing relationships her parents had involved themselves in once they'd begun living in the commune. All she had understood then was that neither her mother nor her father any longer had time for her; other people absorbed their attention and she was left alone.

Later, when she had been entering her teen years, her mother had tried once to explain it to her. 'You see, darling, there are things that make your body feel good in lovely and exciting ways. Those things make you feel good all over, so there's nothing wrong with those things—nothing at all. The trick is not to have hang-ups about that kind of pleasure. There aren't any rules, so you never need to feel there are things you *must* do or *can't* do. You do what you please, which is why I adore living here, and it's going to be even better for *you!*'

'Why?' Anne had asked, a solemn, slender child with wild brown curls and bitter scepticism in her eyes.

'Because I—and your father too, of course—had to learn to get rid of all the hang-ups we'd been taught, and that's sometimes made it. . .oh, just a little difficult. . . But *you*, you lucky girl——' here she had paused to hug Anne briefly to her, one of the few gestures of affection Anne could remember from the years in the commune '—you won't have any of those dreary hang-ups! You've always lived this way, you've seen how these things work. You'll have such fun, darling! It almost makes me jealous that I can't be *you*, and know from the very start that it's all *free!*'

But it wasn't all free; Anne already knew that, because she was the one who had always paid the price of neglect and indifference. She kept on paying the price until she was old enough to leave her parents and the commune. Then, finally independent and able to establish her own standards, she had vowed that she would not live her life the way her parents had been living theirs. It hadn't been easy for her, of course. There had been a lot of men who wanted casual physical relationships with her. Sometimes, she admitted honestly, it was hard to keep refusing them—not because she wanted the physical aspects of a relationship, but because it seemed that no one would ever care about her unless she permitted the physical aspects to occur.

Still, she had held out, trying to believe she would find a man who felt as she did, and the miracle was that she had found Joel. The beauty of their relationship was that he had found her attractive and had cared about her *without* the distractions and complications of physical need. With Joel, Anne had finally found a stable, *safe* relationship; she was building a life with Joel while they shared his dream of providing him with a gallery. Once that was accomplished, Anne knew—although Joel hadn't actually *said* so yet—that they would marry, but for sane and sensible reasons. Joel was like her: unmoved by anything so base and unpredictable as passion—and that made what had happened tonight even worse.

Tonight, Anne concluded, she had simply lost her head. The last twenty-four hours had been, to say the least, difficult and highly charged with emotion. For the first time in over a year, Joel wasn't present to be her anchor; she had suddenly been alone again, and terrifyingly vulnerable. And Nick—who was undoubtedly a past master at the art of seduction, she conceded bitterly—had sensed her vulnerability and had exploited it beyond her wildest imaginings. He had caught her by surprise, unprepared and off balance. Because of that, she had betrayed Joel, if only briefly and only with her body—*not* with her heart and mind! Now she vowed fiercely that it would not happen again.

She would, of course, have to keep playing the game. Nick was right about that: no one would believe they were lovers unless there was some physical contact between them, so she had no choice. The only way to make Joel's dream come true, the only way to redeem herself for him, was to do the job Nick was paying her to do. But the next time he touched her, she would know what to expect, and she would not respond; she would control her feelings and keep them firmly in check. She would be true to Joel after this one brief moment of madness, and what had happened tonight would *never* happen again!

She was wrong. What had happened that night did happen again; it happened each time Nick touched her, and, as the days passed, Anne was finally forced to acknowledge the truth about herself. She was more like her parents than she had known. She shared their fatal flaw of physical need, the flaw which had driven them into meaningless affairs. In spite of her deep and abiding love for Joel, Anne had discovered within herself an appalling weakness, a wild flame which came to life in the arms of a man she despised.

She was like a hostage, she concluded. She was living in a strange and confusing world, left alone during the day while Nick was at work, her isolation only relieved in the evenings, when she was with him. Like a hostage, she was completely dependent on him; like a hostage, she both feared and was drawn to her captor.

When she was with him, Anne was always incredibly aware of Nick, watching him in a way she had never watched Joel. In Nick, she saw a physical magnetism she had never seen in Joel; suddenly even the smallest things about a man assumed an overriding importance to her. When Nick was preoccupied, she studied his long, clever fingers and the way they toyed with an object. When he was impatient or bored, she learned to expect him to pace the room, and she hungrily absorbed the grace of his movements. When she said something to please him, she waited for and then memorised his devastating smile.

She had always known he was an attractive man; now she was obsessed by his dark good looks. It was as though he had impressed his physical presence upon her when he had kissed her that first time. Now Nicholas Thayer and her preoccupation with him threatened to consume her.

The worst of it was that he knew all that. After that first physical encounter, he exploited her reactions; they amused him, and he took pleasure in tormenting her by using them to his advantage. The only saving grace for her was that he never again touched her when they were alone. Then, he treated her as he had at the start: as a casual friend whose conversation entertained him. At those times, Anne could almost pretend that things were as they had been before: that she was spending only the evening with Nick and that, when it was done, she could return to the safe haven Joel had created for her.

But the other, darker side of her relationship with Nick was always there, waiting for the evenings when they went out. When there were other people present, he played the game she both craved and feared. With consummate skill he held her spellbound with his smile for her alone and his slightest touch—those cleverly possessive gestures which converted their relationship into one highly charged with the strange new excitement she was beginning to know too well. Anticipation—even tension—would build within her until he would finally end the suspense.

'Come here, love,' he would murmur, opening his arms to her while others watched with eager curiosity. 'I've waited long enough for you.'

She would try at those times to think of Joel and their love for each other, would try to fight the weakness invading her body, but she always failed. Each time Nick took her into his arms and kissed her, the same spontaneous and uncontrolled response flared within her. She would mould her body into his, her will and her thoughts of Joel consumed by the fire of desire.

Afterwards, of course, when the evening had ended and she was alone in the impersonal beauty of Nick's bedroom, it was guilt which consumed her. She would lie alone in his enormous bed, crying bitter tears—hating him for what he had done to her, hating herself for betraying the precious gift of Joel's love. Each night she would resolve to be better; her resolve would last through the next day—until the evening, when Nick returned to her and the wild longing started again.

CHAPTER FOUR

'HERE.' Nick returned to the penthouse one evening to hand Anne a large manila envelope. 'I've brought you the lease on the gallery and the bankbook I promised you.'

'Thank you,' she said formally, accepting the envelope he forced into her hands, not bothering to open it. 'Shouldn't you keep this until I've finished my job? After all, how do you know you can trust me?'

'I'm a good judge of character,' he explained, sitting with long-limbed grace in the chair opposite hers, a smile playing at the corners of his mouth as he spoke. 'As far as I'm concerned, they already belong to you—not to Joel, you understand. Both the lease and the bank account are in your name alone. If you're wise, you'll keep it that way. I'm a great believer in protecting assets. At the moment, these are all you have——'

'And they're for Joel,' she put in quickly, leaving the room before he could say anything to insult Joel and cause another argument.

The next evening did start with an argument, one caused by the gift he brought her. 'You ought to have jewellery,' he announced, taking her up to the study between their bedrooms and handing her a velvet case. 'These are for you to keep, after you leave. Consider them protection for the future—and for heaven's sake, don't let Joel sell them.'

'I don't need protection and I don't want jewellery,' Anne snapped, then tried for a little diplomacy. 'You've been generous enough.'

'Don't tell me how generous I can be,' Nick said harshly, restlessly prowling the room, 'and don't tell me you don't need protection! You'll need all you can get, until you finally decide to get rid of that——'

'Don't say it! Don't you *dare*,' she raged, trying to force the velvet case back into his hand. 'Don't say *anything* against Joel!'

'All right, I won't.' He capitulated with a disarming grin, shoving his hands into his pockets so that she couldn't give the case back. 'But take the jewellery anyway. Please?' he added, waiting until her stormy expression began to fade. 'You need it, you see—to maintain the illusion. It's like kissing you, or making sure we're seen by people who will carry the word back to Alex and Liv. Jewellery's just another part of the job.'

'It's a pretty strange job, when I get paid for taking jewellery,' she observed, unbending enough to answer his smile with a tentative one of her own, a smile which vanished as soon as she opened the velvet case. There, on creamy white satin, lay an enormous teardrop emerald pendant in an ornate gold setting, with a matching bracelet and drop earrings. Instantly she snapped the case shut, thrusting it back at him. 'My God, Nick! They must be worth a fortune!'

'Hardly that,' he told her, amusement lighting his eyes. 'Take them, Anne. They're yours.'

'But I can't—and they aren't!'

'It's a good thing no one can hear you,' he teased. 'No woman in your position ever turns down a gift like that. Any self-respecting mistress wants all the jewellery she can get!'

'But I'm *not* a self-respecting mistress—if there is such a thing,' she told him, trying not to laugh. 'Isn't that a contradiction in terms?'

'Not in your case, Cool Anne—and please don't start arguing that point with me. Peace, Anne? We've had all the fighting I can take for one evening.'

'I don't believe that for a minute!'

'I know, but it sounded good, didn't it?' he enquired hopefully, regarding her with an expression she decided could only be described as fond. 'Unfortunately, there's no time to argue—or anything else—right now. We've got a party to go to, and I hope you won't mind if I choose your dress.'

'Why tonight?' she asked, even as she accepted his hand on her arm, guiding her towards the bedroom. 'You've never done it before.'

'Tonight's rather important to me, and I want to make sure there's no doubt in *any* mind about us,' Nick explained, searching through her clothes, finally selecting a dress of soft green silk. 'There, this will do,' he decided, handing it to her and then leaving the room.

Perhaps he thought it would do, but when she inspected herself in the mirror, Anne felt all her good humour melting away, replaced by shock and embarrassment. She had tried the dress on only once, when she had modelled it for him, and she had paid no attention to how it looked on her. Now she saw that the slender sheath positively clung to her, emphasising every curve. It was even more daring because of the low bodice, supported by two narrow straps, and the deep slash at the side of the skirt. There was nothing self-respecting about her now, she thought, finally turning away from the mirror and drawing a deep breath as she prepared to face Nick.

'Will I do?' she asked when she found him waiting for her in the study, a remote and distinguished figure in the black and white severity of his evening clothes.

'Of course,' he agreed automatically, even before he had taken a long moment to absorb every detail of her appearance. When he had, she saw the slow spark in his eyes as he smiled. 'Very nice,' he pronounced. 'Lord! You look——'

'Like a rich man's mistress,' Anne supplied resentfully.

'That's right, or you will, when you're wearing the emeralds.' He reached for the velvet case and came towards her, moving with a kind of powerful grace. 'Turn around.'

She obeyed, standing motionless, painfully aware of his clever fingers against her skin as he fastened the pendant around her neck, then clasped the bracelet on her wrist. 'Very nice,' he said again, dropping the earrings into her palm, watching while she put them on. 'What's wrong, Anne?' he asked shrewdly.

'I don't like the jewellery—or the dress.' She shrugged resentfully. 'You've succeeded in making me feel like a kept woman.'

'That's what you are,' he told her with a knowing smile.

'Yes, I know.' She looked away unhappily, wondering what had happened to the liking and the sense of fun and she'd felt between them just a little while ago. The dress was what had happened, she realised; he had chosen this wanton dress for her, forced the jewellery on to her. . . 'And one look at me and everyone else will know just how kept I am.'

'That's right. That's why I'm paying you to wear these jewels.' His clever fingers tangled briefly in the artful disorder of her hair, sweeping it back to linger, toying with one of the earrings. 'And the dress.' He fingered one thin strap, tracing it down, towards the soft swell of her breast.

'Nick, please stop,' she protested, her voice suddenly husky in spite of her best efforts to ignore the fire of his touch.

'And I'm paying you to respond, love,' he murmured, a dangerous light in his eyes as he bent his head to kiss her. 'Although I think you'd do that for free,' he finished, when he was done. 'Wouldn't you?'

'No!'

'Yes,' he contradicted softly, his mouth closing over hers again to prove his point.

This time, his kiss was a deliberate provocation, inciting her response; she knew what he was doing, but knowing didn't help. Damn him! she thought, even as he destroyed her resistance so that her arms slipped around his neck and her body instinctively moulded itself against him. 'You're not fair,' she complained weakly when their kiss had ended. 'Why do you do this?'

'It amuses me,' he told her, laughter lurking at the corners of his mouth. 'Isn't that what you promised me at the start?'

Anne closed her eyes against the sight of him, hating him for the way he could humiliate her with his cool and careless words, for the way he always kept his self-control while demolishing hers. He always had the edge and the advantage, she thought bitterly. Once he had accused her of being the puppet on Joel's string; now he had made her his. 'I didn't mean *this*,' she attempted, and heard his laugh.

'I know, but that's not going to stop me.' He kissed her one last time, then finally released her. 'Nor do you want me to stop,' he mocked. 'You won't admit it, of course, but you've discovered something new about yourself—something you never felt with Joel, something he didn't want you to feel.'

'Something *I* didn't want to feel,' she countered hotly, goaded beyond pretence. 'I knew about this; I saw what it did to my parents, and I didn't want it!'

'No? That's not terribly realistic, Anne,' Nick told her, suddenly serious. 'This feeling exists in everyone, and the trick is to know how to use it and enjoy it—something you're learning now in spite of yourself. Perhaps you would thank me for helping you to complete your education,' he suggested with a surprisingly gentle smile. 'At least I'm willing—as Joel wasn't—to let you grow up. Now, come along,' he commanded, giving her no chance to speak. 'We're already late for the party.'

'Nick darling, I don't believe it!' The redhead, still dazzling despite being well past her prime, greeted him from the far side of the crowded drawing-room.

'That's our hostess, Gloria,' Nick explained to Anne as the redhead threaded her way towards them. 'She's one of Liv's best sources of information.'

'We'd begun to think you were no longer among the living,' Gloria told him as she reached his side, 'but you're looking well—which is more than can be said for your brother. I saw him in Paris three weeks ago, and he was looking positively ghastly. But you'll see that for-yourself in a week or so.'

'Will I?'

'Well, that's what *I've* been told. He's in the American Hospital at the moment—some kind of tests, I believe—but he'll be out in a few days, and he and Liv intend to move on to St Denis as soon as he feels fit to travel. He seems to be looking forward to seeing you—for once in his life. Liv, of course, is too, although she assumed you'd be coming alone.'

'No chance of that,' laughed Nick, drawing Anne forward to introduce her, his hand resting lightly on her shoulder.

'Well. . .' Gloria took her time, absorbing the visual impact of the emeralds and the dress in her inspection of Anne. 'She's not your usual type, is she?'

'That's not a particularly diplomatic question,' Nick countered easily enough, but Anne knew him so well by now that she could tell that the question didn't please him. So Nick had a usual type and he didn't like to be reminded of it, she realised when she glanced up at his face and saw the muscle knotting along the line of his jaw. Still, there was no sign of tension in his voice when he said to Gloria, 'You really don't know anything about my usual type.'

'But I did, Nick. Lord, we all did—some years ago, but it appears that your tastes have changed.' She paused, casting another long appraising look at Anne before turning back to Nick. 'I thought the days were long past when you'd be even temporarily faithful to a woman—*again*,' she finished with a malicious smile.

'But then I met Anne.' For an instant, his grip on her shoulder was painful; then, unexpectedly, his clever fingers were stroking the delicate line of its curve in a sensuously possessive gesture. 'She makes it easy to be faithful,' he explained lightly, but Anne could actually feel the effort that went into the achieving of the effect, 'and infinitely enjoyable.'

'If you say so, darling. At least I'll have the fun of telling Liv about your new toy—and the fun of hearing her reaction.' For a moment, Gloria's gaze followed the movement of his fingers. 'You've certainly given me something to tell, and it will come as a shock, you know. She's convinced that—family loyalty to the contrary—she can have what she wants.'

'She's wrong.'

Gloria laughed. 'Well, you'd like to think so, but I don't think Liv will find it so easy to believe your change of heart.' She drifted away then, leaving that telling phrase hanging in the air.

Even while she and Nick circulated among the other guests, while she chatted and made the usual meaningless small talk, Anne's mind was busy with what Gloria had said. Liv wasn't going to believe Nick's change of heart—towards *Liv*? Anne wondered, glancing up at his dark, aristocratic features. Had he once wanted—even loved—his brother's wife?

Watching him as he moved among these clever and glittering people, his cool self-possession intact, it seemed impossible. Nick was strong, determined, calculating. In his arms, she could be reduced to mindless wanting without Nick ever losing his own self-control. *Nothing* touched Nick—or did it? she wondered, her mind working furiously. There had been that one time when, as he had been explaining why he needed her help to reassure Alex, his composure had slipped. Then, Anne had been pleased to see that she could shake his poise, but she had thought it was only because he was concerned about his brother. Now she wasn't so sure.

Without knowing, had Gloria exposed a deeper, darker truth? Perhaps she had, Anne mused, taking another quick look at Nick's clean and unrevealing profile. After all, for a man with such an air of detachment, his reaction that evening had been out of proportion, almost too strong. Surely it had been greater than that of simple concern for a brother with whom, on Nick's own admission, he hadn't got along for years! So was Nick's problem really with Alex, or with his wife—someone who had once mattered to Nick?

And if the problem was with Alex's wife, what did it matter to Anne? Other than the slight consolation of knowing that Nick was considerably more human—and fallible—than she had thought, what did it matter that he'd once cared for his brother's wife?

And *still did*! Anne suddenly realised, the knowledge like an electric current through her. Gloria might think Nick had had a change of heart; everyone might think that, but Anne knew better. She and Nick were the only ones who knew that their relationship was purely business, which meant—almost probably—that Nick still cared for Liv. Now *that* was something new and different about the intimate stranger standing beside her, his hand resting possessively on her arm. That knowledge might, in ways she couldn't work out now, make a difference between them. Knowing how Nick felt about Liv just might give Anne some kind of edge—if she could only find it!

'So,' she began when they finally had some privacy, when Nick had drawn her into his arms to dance to the slow rhythm of the music, 'tell me about Liv.'

'What about her?' he countered, increasing the contact between them.

'That's what I'd like to know. There's more to this than you've told me.'

'Is there?'

'You know damn well there is,' she whispered fiercely, watching his face and refusing to buy its blandly expressionless mask. 'You were involved with her,' she announced boldly, determined to follow her instinct, 'and I think she still matters to you. Doesn't she, Nick?'

'Where did you get an idea like that?' he enquired, and Anne knew him well enough by now to see that his smile of tolerant amusement didn't quite come off. 'She's an attractive woman—nothing more.'

'But Gloria said——'

'You shouldn't listen to Gloria,' he cautioned—just a little too quickly. 'Gloria talks a lot of nonsense.'

'Not in this case.' She was right! Anne thought, exulting in the knowledge. Finally, after all this time of being his dependant, his hostage, she had been given a weapon to use against him, a way to fight back when he used her feelings against her. But her knowledge was more than a weapon, she discovered when she smiled up at him. It had made him more human, made her feel like more of a person when she was with him. She wasn't his equal, of course. He would never let her be that, but they might *meet* as equals—at least on occasion, and that was a curiously liberating thought. 'I think I've found a chink in your armour, Nicholas Thayer,' she teased now, meeting his hooded gaze. 'It's your brother's wife, isn't it? You wanted her once, and you still do!'

'I'm not sure.' It wasn't quite an admission, but against his will she had driven him to reveal something profound about himself. 'It's been years since I've seen her.'

'But she mattered to you then?'

'Yes! Satisfied?' he demanded harshly.

'Not really satisfied, but it's good to know that you're not always this super-controlled and rational man,' she explained, feeling a real sense of power for the first time since their strange arrangement had begun. More than that, she discovered, she was *liking* him better—more than she had ever liked him before. Knowing that she could be his occasional equal, understanding that he really was flesh and blood—that he was vulnerable to *someone*, even if not to her—made him seem more like her friend than her master. As though the two of them were in this together, she realised with real pleasure. 'Dear Nick,' she said, favouring him with a brilliant smile, 'you've got a weakness too.'

'Is that so important to you?'

'Yes! I'll remember it whenever you start exploiting *my* weakness.' She slipped her arms around his neck, deliberately pressing herself against him. 'What do you do at moments like this?' she asked, revelling in the knowledge that for once she had the upper hand. Perhaps, in his own way, he was as disturbed and confused as she was, and was finding this bizarre arrangement between them just as difficult to handle. 'Poor Nick,' she continued, looking up at him, torn between sympathy and satisfaction, understanding and unholy glee, 'do you find that this isn't as easy as *you* thought it would be? When you kiss me, do you have to pretend that I'm Liv?'

'No,' he answered with an unreadable smile. 'It's possible for there to be physical attraction without any real feeling.'

'I know. You've taught me that.' She permitted her fingers to brush lightly through his hair. 'And it's time to let it happen again—my love,' she mocked. 'Gloria's watching us like a hawk. If you want her to have something to tell your brother—and Liv, of course— you'd better kiss me.'

'If you insist,' he murmured, and his mouth closed over hers with a fierce possessiveness that was far more than an attempt to maintain the illusion. It was part punishment, part desperation and—either way—Anne had the satisfaction of knowing that she had finally goaded him beyond the limits of his self-control.

'We're well off the beaten track here,' Nick explained as the little six-seater plane landed at the small airfield on St Denis. 'We get very few tourists, and I'm afraid you won't find much excitement.'

'I expect I'll find plenty,' Anne told him as she stepped from the plane into a perfect dream of a summer day, 'what with one thing and another,' she added, glancing back at him to make sure he got her point.

The balance of their relationship had shifted, the night she had learned the truth about Liv. During the ride from the landing field to Nick's cottage, while Nick kept up a steady conversatin with Kitt, their loquacious driver, Anne reflected on the changes. She was no longer

Nick's puppet, no longer at the mercy of his subtle torment. Now she gave as good as she got, touching a nerve in him each time she mentioned Liv's name. They were equals now, neither of them entirely in control of their relationship, neither entirely in control of the other.

'Here it is, Nick,' said Kitt as he made the turn from the unpaved road on to a narrower, rougher track. 'You've probably forgotten what it looks like after all time—nearly three years since you last came down.'

'I've been busy,' Nick explained briefly, his hand resting lightly on Anne's shoulder.

'Sure you have,' Kitt agreed with a scepticism that suggested years of friendship, 'but that never used to keep you away.'

'Things change.'

'Sure they do,' Kitt allowed cheerfully. 'Now you've got yourself a pretty lady. If she likes it here, maybe you'll come back more often.'

'Maybe so.' Nick smiled at Anne, and she had to admire the way he was creating the illusion. 'I'll try to see that she enjoys herself. That's the best way to make sure she wants to come back.'

The narrow track wound gradually uphill, exotic trees on either side forming a deep green tunnel. At the top of the hill, they came into a clearing of lush green lawns and flowering shrubs. The air was heavy with the mingled scents of flowers and salt water, and Anne inhaled deeply, struck by the contrast between this place and the cold, grey January day they had left behind in New York. Against the sudden vivid blue of the sea, she saw what appeared to be a collection of ramshackle, rough-shingled sheds, connected to one another by a wide veranda.

'All ready for you, Nick,' Kitt told him, stopping in front of a wide open door. 'Mr Bill was staying here, but we cleared him out and sent him up to the big house yesterday, when Mr Alex and his wife arrived. They want you for dinner tonight, but Mr Alex says he's so tired that you can't stay late.' Kitt shook his head. 'That man surely does enjoy poor health! None of it real, if you want my opinion, but try telling him that.'

He and Nick carried in the luggage while Anne followed more slowly, looking around. Inside, the cottage was light and surprisingly spacious, a U-shaped structure with one room flowing naturally into another. In marked contrast to the New York penthouse, this place was casual and easy, with no attempt to keep to one style of décor. The furniture was a haphazard collection of antique and modern, and the walls were hung with an oddly assorted mixture of seascapes and antique Japanese screens.

On the outer walls of the U-shape, wide, unscreened doors served as both windows and access to the veranda. On the inner walls were identical doors, opening on to small porches, overlooking what appeared to be—incredibly—a naturally formed pool. It was edged with rough boulders and an untamed growth of ferns and flowering shrubs.

'Nick!' Anne called, following him into the bedroom and staring disapprovingly at the pool. 'Is that a swimming pool?'

'I'm afraid so—complete with chlorine and filtration system. Why? Don't you like it?'

'It seems a bit contrived. I gather that you just dive through the door of whatever room you're in when you decide to go swimming. It's an example of conspicious consumption, if I ever saw one!'

'And you're a spoilsport, love,' he smiled, catching her to him. 'First you don't like my place in New York, and now there's something wrong here. Are you ever satisfied?'

'On occasion,' she teased, aware that Kitt was following their exchange with considerable interest. '*You* satisfy me—on occasion,' she added for good measure.

'OK, Nick,' Kitt broke in cheerfully. 'Do you want me to send Winnie down to unpack for you?'

'Give us a few minutes,' Nick told him, releasing Anne to shed his jacket and loosen his tie. 'Anne can dig out our bathing suits, and we'll change and have a swim. Which will it be, love? The pool or the sea?'

'The sea, of course,' she answered promptly. 'I'll save the pool for a time when I haven't the energy to walk farther than the nearest door.'

'Stop making fun of my swimming pool.' He turned her to face him, his fingers finding the zipper at the back of her dress while his mouth began to move on hers.

She started to protest, and instantly his mouth closed over hers, silencing her with the authority of his kiss. She was crushed against him, his left arm around her waist and his right splayed against her back, cool against her heated skin. As she began to respond to his touch and the insidious pleasure of his kiss, his hold slackened and she felt his fingers working at the hooks fastening her bra. What did Kitt think of this? she wondered distractedly as she finally heard the sound of his retreating footsteps.

'Nick, stop it!' She wrenched herself away, just as he succeeded in unhooking her bra. 'Undressing me isn't part of our bargain!'

'I didn't undress you,' he pointed out, moving away to begin hunting through the suitcases. 'I merely started the process—and only for Kitt's benefit. The servants here gossip like mad, and we might as well make it clear from the outset that I find it difficult to keep my hands off you—and that you like it,' he added with a knowing smile, tossing her two scraps of green and pale yellow fabric. 'Here, put this on. You can change in the bathroom if you like.'

'Of course I like,' she snapped, clutching the bikini, her shoulders braced to hold her dress more or less in place. 'You're going to change here, I suppose.'

'That's right. We'll be living a little more in each other's pockets here, and you'd better get used to the idea. I'll sleep in a little spare bedroom on the lower level, but I'll be changing here.'

'Or in the bathroom,' she suggested pointedly, hastily

retreating when he started to unbutton his shirt. 'Knock when you're decent.'

'Watch it, love! That's supposed to be my line,' he called after her as she closed and locked the bathroom door.

When she emerged, ten minutes later, the sight of him in bathing briefs was enough to make her pulse race. She'd known he was powerfully built, but she wasn't prepared for the impact of his broad shoulders, the flat planes of his stomach, his lean hips and strongly muscled legs. God, he was handsome, she thought, feeling dazed, and she might have continued to stare at him indefinitely, if he hadn't broken the spell by speaking.

'Very nice,' he observed, casually inspecting her bikini-clad figure before leading the way down to the beach.

It was an ideal setting, she saw, admiring the crescent of brilliant white sand, ringed on the landward side by more lush vegetation. Graceful palm trees framed the view up a gentle rise to where a large white house lay gleaming in the afternoon sun.

'Is that Alex's place?' she asked, shading her eyes to get a better look at it.

'Yes. It belonged to my grandmother, who left it to him. It's an old planter's mansion—lovingly restored, as the saying goes, but not to my taste.'

'Why not?'

'I don't know. I spent much of my childhood there, but I never felt I belonged.' Nick shrugged—uncomfortably, Anne thought, as though he had revealed too much—then suddenly caught her to him.

'What are you doing?' she demanded.

'What do you think?' He pulled her even closer. 'Kissing you for our admiring audience.'

'I don't see an audience,' she objected half-heartedly, distracted by the contact between his warm flesh and her own.

'But they see us,' said Nick, smiling down at her.

'Without a doubt, the servants are watching, possibly Alex or Liv too. Put your arms around me, Anne.'

He didn't need to tell her. She could think of nothing she wanted more, and she was already reaching for him. Her lips parted the instant he kissed her, permitting him to probe and tease until she heard her own muffled sigh of pleasure and her hands convulsively gripped his shoulders.

'Nicely done, love,' he told her, his own self-possession intact when he released her. 'Now let's go swimming.'

'I think. . .I'd rather not,' she said unevenly, shaken by the depth of her response, so aware of her body's craving for his that she couldn't feel entirely safe with him now. She needed distance, she knew, a little time to gather her scattered wits. 'You go. I'll stay here and rest.'

'If you like,' he agreed, watching with a knowing smile while she spread out one of the towels and lay down, burying her face in her arms in an attempt to hide the colour staining her cheeks. 'You're going to burn,' he warned, and she felt his strongly muscled thigh brushing her hip when he knelt beside her. 'I'd better put some lotion on you.'

He was close—too close—and she fought against the sudden assault to her senses when she felt his fingers working at the strings holding her bikini top in place. 'Please don't,' she whispered, afraid to move. 'I can do that myself.'

'You can't do your own back.' The strings fell away and he began to rub lotion into her heated skin, working with even, almost impersonal movements, taking absolutely no advantage of her near-nakedness. 'You see?' he teased when he was done, 'you were worrying about nothing at all, but you really *can* relax now. I'll be in the water—and out of harm's way!'

This wasn't going to be easy, Anne brooded when he was gone. They hadn't been on the island an hour, and there had already been too much intimacy between them—more than she thought she could handle. Somehow she'd lost the edge she had acquired at Gloria's party, and she wasn't sure how she could get it back. Maintaining the balance wasn't going to be easy in this exotic setting, where she was so terribly far away from Joel. . .

'Joel.' She whispered his name against the soft murmur of the waves, trying to summon his image. Joel was the cool one, the one who steadied her. . .which was strange, she mused. It ought to be the other way round. Nick, after all, was the cold and pragmatic businessman; *he* shouldn't have the ability to raise her emotions to a fever pitch. Some time—when she wasn't so tired, perhaps—she'd have to try to understand why it was that he moved her so. . .

She must have drifted off, because she didn't realise Nick had returned until she felt his cool kiss on her cheek. 'It's you,' she said stupidly, turning her head to find him beside her. Fascinated, she saw the fine beading of salt water on his skin, then was dazzled when he shifted slightly and the droplets were caught by the sun to glitter against his deep tan. Think of Joel! she urged herself, but Joel was far away and Nick was *here*, his lean, hard body so close to hers. . .'Your hands are cold,' she complained, turning away from him to avoid his touch, shivering when his arms closed around her and he drew her back against the cool length of his body. 'You're cold all over!'

'And you're warm,' he teased, scattering light kisses along the curve of her shoulder while his hands moved higher, coming to rest just beneath the swell of her breasts. 'Won't you warm me, Anne?'

'I. . .no, please don't, Nick,' she objected weakly, but it was already too late. This all felt so good, she admitted to herself, absorbed by the length of his body, cool against hers, and his lips on her skin. 'We shouldn't do this,' she whispered, even as she stirred, instinctively seeking more contact between them.

'It's all right, love.' She sighed in protest when he

released her to retie her bikini top, then felt him turning her to face him, gathering her body to his. 'This is part of the game,' he explained, his lips seeking hers with maddening deliberation. 'Someone's coming.'

Thank goodness! she thought distractedly, wrapping her arms around him as the last of her resolution slipped away. Someone coming meant that this couldn't last much longer, but for now—until that someone arrived to save her—she couldn't help herself. She shifted impatiently, parting her lips as her fingers curled into his damp hair to pull him closer.

'Hello. Am I interrupting something important?'

Anne froze when she heard the lightly accented voice, heard Nick swear under his breath as he abruptly released her.

'Lord, Liv! You picked the damnedest time to come for a swim,' he said unevenly. 'Couldn't you have waited a while?'

'Sorry, darling, but I didn't come for a swim. I came to see you, and you might be a little more pleasant about it. After all, it's been three years.'

Anne drew a deep breath, struggling to regain her composure as she sat up to confront the woman who had created the need for her presence here, the woman whose arrival on the beach had undoubtedly prompted Nick's clever lovemaking of a moment before. So this was Liv, Anne thought, facing the incredibly beautiful woman.

Liv's hair was long and very straight, such a pale gold that the colour had to be real. Surely no woman would have the courage to fake such an improbable shade! She was tall, her figure set off to perfection by the minimal blue bikini she wore. Her eyes were a deep and vivid matching blue, and her complexion was flawless. When she smiled, as she did now, she fairly glowed, suggesting an odd combination of childlike high spirits and provocative sexuality.

'Anyway, darling, I'm happy to see *you*, even if you do choose to be less than gracious.' Liv spread out her towel and sat down next to Nick, leaning forward until her barely clad breasts brushed lightly against his chest as she kissed his cheek. 'Is that Anne?'

'Of course it is,' Nick said coldly, shifting away from Liv to put his hand on Anne's shoulder in what was either a possessive or protective gesture.

Hateful woman! Anne thought viciously, enduring the disdainful inspection of those cold blue eyes. She supposed Liv intended her to feel awkward or embarrassed; instead, she was merely angry.

'Well, she's attractive enough, I suppose,' Liv concluded after a moment, turning her attention back to Nick, 'but not precisely the type I'd have expected you to choose. I understand she was living with an artist before you picked her up.'

'A dealer, actually.' When Anne spoke before Nick could, Liv subject her to an even colder stare.

'I stand corrected—not that it makes any difference.' She reached for the tube of sun-screen lying on Nick's towel, pouring some into her hand. 'I'll bet she just jumped at the chance to move in with you, darling,' she observed, beginning to stroke the lotion on to her skin, her hand moving slowly, with deliberate sensuality. 'After a starving artist—or dealer—you can offer so much more in the way of financial rewards, can't you?'

'You would think of that,' Nick said sourly, his fingers involuntarily tensing against Anne's shoulder.

'But I didn't,' Anne contributed, lying through her teeth. 'You can't seriously believe that finances had anything to do with my wanting to be with Nick!' With considerably more daring than she had known she possessed she half turned to him, resting her hand on his chest in a possessive gesture of her own. 'Money had nothing to do with it. I just couldn't resist him, you see. I don't think any woman could.'

'I see.' Liv bit out the words, and Anne had the satisfaction of seeing the older woman momentarily off balance. 'Do you think she loves you, Nick?'

'Liv's always like this,' he told Anne, ignoring Liv while his hand closed over hers to press it even closer to his flesh. Only then did he look back at Liv. 'At the risk of sounding as rude as you've been, that's none of your business.'

'If you say so, darling.' Liv bent her head, her hair falling forward in a shimmering wave, calling attention to her hand as it moved in a caressing sweep to smooth lotion on to one long, golden leg. 'It's not that I really care, you understand. I was only trying to make conversation.' She was silent for a moment, her hand continuing its hypnotic movements. 'Alex is resting—which is what he does best—and Bill has gone out somewhere. I'm starved for conversation and when I saw you down here, I thought—thank God, someone to talk to.'

'You should have called one of your friends,' Nick suggested coolly, but Anne saw that his eyes were following the movements of Liv's hand with a kind of hungry absorption. 'There are plenty of them on the island.'

'Ah, but that's not the same, darling Nick.' Unexpectedly, she looked up, grinning when she saw the look in his eyes. 'You and I—we're such old friends, darling.' Very deliberately she lifted her hand from her leg to rest it on his arm. 'You know that the others don't mean nearly as much. Perhaps that's because we're family,' she finished with a malicious smile.

'I doubt it.' Nick seemed more in possession of his emotions now, and he ignored her hand to turn back to Anne with a lazy smile. 'Now that the beach is so crowded, shall we go back to the cottage? We've got a few hours until dinner—time enough to finish what we started here.'

'Hardly subtle, Nick,' Liv observed drily, withdrawing her hand.

'But I'm not in the mood to be subtle, Liv. I'm in the mood for something else entirely.'

'Then perhaps I'll see you at dinner,' snapped Liv, her deep blue eyes alive with anger as she watched Nick stand up and offer his hand to Anne. 'Or perhaps I won't,' she added coldly, making it sound like both a threat and a challenge, punishing Nick—or daring him to deny that he cared.

'Liv went out,' Alex Thayer announced as he haltingly entered the imposing drawing-room of the big house. 'She's gone for the evening, but at least you got to see her on the beach this afternoon. She's bored, of course. It's been difficult for her since my illnes began—so little for her to do, no parties, no fun. . .' He trailed off, a pale and fretful copy of his brother, with none of Nick's muscular authority. Alex's features were softer and less emphatic and set in what appeared to be perpetual lines of discontent, his hair was a nondescript shade of brown, streaked with grey. The contrast between the two men was even greater because of Alex's invalid status, obvious in his grey pallor and his expression of weary displeasure. Even his eyes were lifeless and limpid, his gaze resting on Anne without expression when Nick introduced her.

'Yes, of course,' Alex nodded vaguely. 'I'd heard about you, and Liv said she'd seen you. My wife's incredibly lovely, don't you think?' he asked Anne, continuing without waiting for her answer. 'She craves excitement, deserves the proper setting to display her beauty, but it's been months since I've been able to give her that. Now that we're here, I hope she can find ways to amuse herself. But I must sit down.' He smiled apologetically, easing himself into a large wing chair. 'It's my back. . .so painful when I stand. Janet, would you help?' he called, and Anne noticed the woman who had been hovering in the doorway. 'Janet's my nurse,' Alex explained, almost animated for the first time. 'I can't think how I managed without her.'

She was about thirty, Anne guessed, a pretty but unassuming woman in a simple cotton shift. As soon as Alex spoke, she came forward to place a small pillow at his back. She was clearly devoted to her patient, fussing with the pillow until Alex finally pronounced himself satisfied.

'Yes, that's better,' he nodded, accepting her attention

with the wan enthusiasm of a man who enjoyed being ill. 'I've been so much more comfortable since I've had Janet to help me,' he explained, favouring her with a faint smile before gesturing to indicate that the others might sit. 'Do you like it here on St Denis, Anne?'

'Yes,' she answered briefly. Then, of necessity, she was forced to wait while a servant passed drinks—sherry for Anne and Janet, a whisky for Nick and spring water for Alex. 'It's a pleasant change from winter in New York.'

'Yes, of course,' Alex agreed vaguely, then continued with a shade more enthusiasm, 'Liv loves the sun. She was miserable in Paris—the cold and the damp. She couldn't wait to be here, and I have great hopes for my own health now. What do you do, Anne?' he asked in another of his abrupt shifts.

'I——' Anne stopped as she realised that she had no real purpose, wouldn't have one until she went back to Joel.

'She pleases me,' Nick answered for her, sensing her difficulty.

'Not an easy task,' Alex observed drily, and then turned back to Nick. 'Your taste must have changed. She's quite different from the type you've favoured in the past.'

'I decided that the time had come to find someone with a little more substance. Among other things, she's got a sense of humour, and she's not afraid of me.'

'That can't be easy to manage—living with you all the time. You have my smypathy, Anne,' Alex continued, directing his attention to her once again. 'And what about Nick? Does he please you?'

None of your damn business! she was tempted to say, but she hesitated, playing for time by staring down at her glass. There were so many undercurrents here; Alex was a past master at them. This pale and fretful imitation of Nick wasn't a very nice person, and he was one of life's takers—a spoiler and a parasite. She wouldn't have cared what she told him except that she cared about doing what Nick expected of her. 'Of course he pleases me,' she responded at last. How could he not? He's everything *you're* not! she added to herself. But that was a dangerous thought, she realised instantly. It confused her, so for her own protection she added quickly, 'At least, he does most of the time.'

'That's a surprise. Nick's usually so abrasive—one of the most difficult people I've ever known. When we were children, he never got along with anyone. My grandmother had to send him away to boarding school to be done with his everlasting arguments. Still, he must be easier on women than on family. He's certainly successful at attracting them.'

'Has Anne mellowed you, do you think?' Alex asked Nick over dinner. 'Has she smoothed down some of your sharper edges?'

'I doubt it.'

'Yes, so do I.' Alex hesitated, nervously fingering his fork while Janet anxiously watched. 'Still, perhaps we could try, Nick,' he resumed. 'We've seen so little of each other these past few years. Perhaps it's because I've been ill so much—so many different things. . .I've begun to want more of a sense of belonging to something; I'd like to feel I had a family, and I thought perhaps we could finally be friends.'

'There's no reason why we can't be,' said Nick, and Anne wondered if Alex heard the shading of caution in his brother's voice. 'Whatever you want, Alex.'

'I don't know what I want.' Alex gestured with nervous impatience, and Janet again grew anxious. 'That's what happens whenever I see you. It's your attitude,' he continued petulantly, while Anne clenched her hands beneath the edge of the table, possessed by a sudden fierce impulse to slap him. 'Because of you, I've always felt so useless and indecisive, and that's become even worse because of all these health problems of mine. I've done almost nothing for nearly a year—no parties, no amusing trips with Liv. . . It's been hell, and I don't know what I want any more.'

'Perhaps parties and trips aren't enough,' Nick suggested carefully.

'That's all I have. There's nothing else I can do,' Alex countered with surprising fierceness. 'It's always suited me very well, but I can't enjoy myself when I'm in the hospital or trying to rest and regain my strength. I've been so useless for so long, and all this inactivity is bad for me. And now you try to tell me that the things I can enjoy aren't enough, and that doesn't help at all. Couldn't you try to be kind? Take an interest in me?'

'In what way, Alex?' Nick asked gently, trying tact and kindness on a man who demanded both but, Anne could see, actually wanted neither emotion. 'We don't have a great deal in common.'

'There you go,' Alex complained fretfully, reading what he wanted into Nick's words, clearly happier being miserable. 'You will persist in treating me with sarcasm, and that only makes things harder for me. I can't be blamed for the fact that you inherited the business, but that left me with nothing to do. I know you don't think so, but I hate having nothing to do.'

'Have you ever considered working? It might——'

'Grandmother didn't raise me to work,' Alex snapped, then leaned back in his chair, closing his eyes while Anne fought a second impulse to slap the man. 'Perhaps it wasn't a wise idea for the two of us to be together, but I felt I had to do something. I feel so alone.'

'You're not alone, Alex,' Nick reminded him. 'You have Liv.'

'But that's not the same.' Alex sighed and then opened his eyes, catching Janet's worried gaze. 'Yes, I know,' he said to her with the faintest of smiles, 'I'm upsetting myself, and it's not good for me.'

'I'm afraid you've become too tired. You've been up far too long, Mr Thayer.'

'Yes. . .yes, of course.' Cautiously, he stood up, then

braced himself against the table. 'That explains everything, Nick—why I've been so irritable with you. If I can get enough rest and begin to feel better, can we try again? I don't want you to hold this evening against me.'

'I won't.' Nick got to his feet, briefly clasping his brother's hand. 'I've never held anything against you,' he said with strange intensity. 'I wish you'd believe that. We'll try again when you're feeling better.'

CHAPTER FIVE

EVEN though there were things she would have liked to say, Anne had been a silent observer of the bizarre exchange between Nick and Alex. She had waited, withholding all her pithy comments, until the two of them were walking back to his cottage. Then she spoke her mind.

'Whatever is wrong with your brother, your grandmother certainly had a lot to do with it.'

'What do you mean?' asked Nick after a moment, as though his thoughts had been far away.

'She didn't raise him to *work*, for heaven's sake! What did she raise him to do, I wonder? And where were your parents, that they weren't raising him themselves?'

'She was raising him to be a gentleman, I suppose,' he answered, taking her questions in order, 'and he and I are only half-brothers. My father divorced his mother to marry mine. She didn't want another woman's brat around—or so I'm told. Alex went to live with Grandmother, who was delighted with the arrangement.'

'If your mother didn't want him, why didn't his own mother raise him?' Anne persisted. 'I should think that would have made more sense, and Alex might have turned out better.'

'Alex's mother was out of the picture. My father didn't want her to have him. He made sure he got custody.'

'And then didn't keep him? Just shipped a little boy off to live with a grandmother who obviously had some strange ideas?' Anne digested that as they climbed the shallow steps and entered the cottage. 'It's no wonder Alex has problems! Your grandmother didn't raise him to be a gentleman; she raised him to be a playboy, and he compounded the problem by marrying a woman with the morals of an alley-cat.'

She followed Nick into the shadowy living-room, watching as he cast off his white dinner jacket and loosened his tie. 'It's a wonder you turned out so well!'

'What makes you think that I did?' he asked with cool irony, pouring himself a drink.

'I know you did, and so do you! You're not a playboy, you're not a neurotic hypochondriac, and, although you may find the type attractive, you didn't marry a tramp like Liv.'

'No, I didn't do that, did I?'

Anne heard the odd inflection in his voice, but chose to ignore it. 'I'd say you turned out very well—under the circumstances.'

'Are you damning me with faint praise?'

'Perhaps,' she grinned. 'You're not perfect, but I suppose that's to be expected—given a family that must be even crazier than mine. It must have been hell for you.'

'Feeling sorry for me, Anne?'

'Yes, but not *much*!'

'Of course not. That would be against your principles.' He smiled at her over the rim of his glass. 'Still, after weeks of sniping at me, it's pleasant to have you on my side for a change.' He finished his drink and set down the glass. 'You have unexpected depths, Anne, and you've been a great help today,' he said softly, taking her hands in his. 'Did you know just how difficult this day was for me?'

'No. . .yes,' she answered distractedly as he increased the pressure on her hands, drawing her towards him. 'What are you doing?'

'Saying thank you,' he murmured, bending his head towards hers.

'There's no need for that!' She snatched her hands away and retreated a step.

'What's the matter, Anne? Don't you want to let me touch you now? Afraid that you might let things go too far at a dangerous time of night?'

'No!'

'Liar!' He laughed. 'You don't trust yourself.'

'And you flatter yourself,' she retorted. 'If there were a door in this damn place, I'd slam it in your face. I'm going to bed now.'

'To lie awake?' he enquired as his parting shot. 'Thinking about what you're missing?'

Anne refused to dignify that with an answer, but she knew he was at least partially right. She had to force herself *not* to think about kissing him or being held in his arms, and the effort kept her awake for a very long time.

Nick *was* kissing her, but this kiss was so different from the others that Anne knew it was only a dream. His mouth was moving on hers with gentle deliberation, kindling no quick flare of passion this time. Instead, she felt a deliciously warm and pleasant lethargy stealing over her, and she lacked the will to fight her imagination. As her lips parted beneath the subtle pressure of his, she comforted herself with the knowledge that this was only a dream. She couldn't be blamed for a dream—not even Joel could blame her for dreaming!—and this felt so good. . .

'Anne? Time to wake up, love. That must have been quite a dream,' he observed as her eyes flew open and she stared up at him in confusion. 'You're blushing.'

'I. . .oh!' This was awful, she thought, instantly wide awake. Nick was lying beside her, propped up on one elbow, his chest a broad expanse of hard lean flesh, his tan very dark against the pale sheets. 'You're not supposed to be in bed with me,' she said fiercely, blushing again as he reached out to pull one of the straps of her nightgown back on to her shoulder. 'What are you *doing* here?'

'Watching you,' he explained with a lazy smile, looking half asleep himself, she thought—his hair casually disordered, his body relaxed and very much at ease next to hers. 'I've been waiting for you to wake up—and don't worry, love,' he told her, his voice an intimate and

sleepy drawl. 'I can't possibly ravage you now. Winnie's
in the kitchen.'

'Who's Winnie?'

'Kitt's wife. When I'm here, she comes every morning
to make breakfast and pick up after me.'

'That still doesn't give you the right——'

'Not so loud, love,' Nick interrupted pleasantly. 'Out-
rage at finding me in bed with you is no way to play the
game—which *is*, after all, what I'm paying you to do.'

'I don't care,' she snapped, but she did lower her voice
to a fierce whisper. 'That still doesn't give you any right
to be naked in bed with me.'

'I'm wearing bathing trunks,' he protested, making a
show of injured dignity. 'I'm as decently dressed as I
was yesterday afternoon on the beach—or would it have
been better not to remind you of yesterday afternoon?'
he queried when he saw the expression on her face.
'What's the matter, Anne? Is this all just a little more
complicated than you thought it would be?'

'It is at the moment!'

'And you're blushing again,' he noted, idly twisting a
strand of her hair between his fingers. 'What were you
dreaming about, that you woke up blushing?'

'I don't remember.'

'No?' he asked sceptically, his grip on her hair holding
her in place when she tried to turn away.

'No! I don't know.' That, at least, was a little closer
to the truth, Anne told herself as he relented, releasing
her hair so that she could turn away from him to bury
her face in the pillow. She had no idea if what she
remembered had been a dream, reality, or a blending of
the two. If Nick *hadn't* kissed her while she was sleeping,
then asking him would mean giving herself away. 'I wish
you wouldn't,' she told him, her voice muffled by the
pillow.

'Wouldn't what?' The bed shifted and he was suddenly
closer, his breath stirring her hair. 'Wouldn't ask you
about your dream?'

'Wouldn't do this!' She stiffened as he swept back her

hair and his lips touched the sensitive spot just behind her ear. 'Nick, please don't!'

'Relax, love,' he murmured, his lips flickering lightly against her skin. 'I'm just playing the game, and I hear Winnie coming.'

If he did, his hearing was better than hers, she thought, the resentment she had felt rapidly fading. His lips were on her shoulder now, his arm around her waist to draw her back against the hard line of his body. 'Nick, please,' she whispered without much conviction, then went limp with relief as she heard footsteps just outside the bedroom door.

'And you didn't believe me,' he teased, straightening up to call out, 'Don't bother to knock, Winnie. It's safe to come in.'

'Safe enough for an old married lady like me? Well, it could be worse, I suppose,' Winnie observed from the doorway. 'It's no more than I expected—to find you and your lady in bed. I brought coffee.'

'Give it to Anne,' Nick said casually. 'She's still half asleep. I've been trying to get her to swim with me, but I've obviously got to go by myself.'

Anne forced herself to turn over as she felt him get up from the bed. 'You're going to dive out of the bedroom into the pool, I suppose.'

'That's right,' he agreed with an unrepentant smile, explaining to Winnie, 'She doesn't approve of my pool.'

'It's decadent!'

'But convenient,' he called back to her just before he executed a clean dive and struck out for the far end of the pool.

'It's absurd,' Anne added for her own benefit, her eyes following him until she remembered Winnie. 'Hello,' she said shyly. 'I'm Anne.'

'I know.' Winnie was an impressive figure, far larger than her husband and even more formidable now, as she studied Anne in minute detail. 'Kitt told me all about you.'

'Oh.' Nervously, Anne twisted the hem of the sheet,

wondering why she should care so much more about Nick's servant's opinion of her than those of his brother and sister-in-law. 'I suppose you don't approve of me—of this. . .'

'I could say that it's not my place to approve or disapprove,' Winnie began carefully, then surprised Anne by smiling broadly, 'but that's what a servant would say, and I've never felt like Nick's servant. I've been more mother than maid, but since I'm not really his mother, I don't have to worry about how things ought to be.

'Let me tell you, Miss Anne,' she continued, surprising Anne once again as she sat down on the edge of the bed, 'if you please Nick—if you make him happy—I'll be satisfied. There's been little enough in his life for him to be happy about, and no one knows that better than Kitt and I. We raised him—to the extent that he got raised at all. The boss lady couldn't be bothered to do the job——'

'His grandmother?' Anne put in quickly.

Winnie nodded. 'As far as she was concerned, the sun rose and set on Mr Alex. She couldn't be bothered with Nick, so when he was here we did our best.'

'Someone throw me a towel,' called Nick, climbing out of the pool on to the narrow porch just outside the open door. 'And the two of you might stop gossiping long enough for Winnie to get breakfast on the table.'

'Nick,' Anne began later, when they had finished a lazy meal on the veranda overlooking the sea, 'why didn't your parents raise *you*?'

'Winnie certainly covered a lot of ground while I was in the pool,' he observed, an edge to his voice. 'I should have made you come with me.'

'She didn't say very much,' Anne defended.

'I'd have been happier if she'd said nothing.'

'Why?'

'I prefer to keep my life as private as possible,' he answered coolly.

He *couldn't* mean that! she thought, staring incredulously across the table at him. True, theirs was only a business arrangement, but he'd *made* her a part of his personal life! Now it rankled that he thought he could involve her so deeply in some parts and completely exclude her from others. In fact, it didn't just rankle; it downright hurt! 'Nick, be real,' she protested hiding her feelings behind a forced laugh. 'You can't drop me into the absolute middle of your life and expect to keep anything private!'

'No? No,' he admitted grudgingly, 'I suppose I can't.'

'Then why didn't your parents raise you?' she repeated.

'My mother died—the only one of my father's wives he didn't divorce.' He got up from the table to lean against the railing, his back to her as he stared out at the sea. 'Wife number three felt very much as my mother had about another woman's brat, so I was sent to join Alex.'

'And that terrible grandmother,' she supplied, forgetting her own hurt as she considered the stark and unhappy childhood lurking behind his cool, unemotional recital.

'Well, not really terrible. Foolish, perhaps, or misguided, but she did give me a home.'

'She gave you a *house*, a roof over your head, and not much of that!' Perhaps she was being too partisan, but— for the moment, at least—she didn't care. If Nick wasn't going to display any emotion over his thoroughly unsatisfactory childhood, she'd do it *for* him! 'Now I know what Alex was talking about when he said you were sent off to boarding school, and Winnie told me that she and Kitt did most of the job of raising you. *That's* a home, but you can't have been here very often. It's no way for a child to live!'

'Yes. . .I know.' Nick stood motionless for another moment, then turned back to her. 'You're a strange girl,' he mused, his expression unreadable, 'and I'm not sure——' He stopped abruptly. When he continued, his tone was very different, and it was obvious that he had censored himself. 'Well, I'm not sure about a lot of things. Look, I've got to make a few calls. Can you amuse yourself for an hour or so?'

'So you *do* exist! I wasn't sure whether to believe the talk or not.'

It was nearly noon when Anne heard the strange voice above the sound of Nick's, still busy on the telephone in the study off the bedroom. She had long since changed into a bikini and taken her sketchbook with her on to the veranda. Now she looked up to see that she was being examined by a young man in white shorts and a deep blue polo shirt. A smaller, slightly less impressive version of Nick, she decided.

'You must be Anne, and I'm Bill—Nick's baby brother.' He smiled engagingly and pulled up a chair. 'Where is old Nick, by the way?'

'On the telephone,' Anne explained, returning his smile.

'Business as usual, I suppose, and more fool he—to abandon such a delectable morsel. And don't worry,' he continued, reading her suddenly wary expression, 'I know you belong to Nick, but there's no reason why I can't look—so long as I remember not to touch. Nick doesn't like other men to poach on his territory. Damn! I put that badly, didn't I?' he asked, smiling apologetically. 'I'm forever saying things I shouldn't, but nobody takes any notice. I'm the grey sheep of the family.'

'The *grey* sheep?'

'Well, I fall in the middle—neither fish nor fowl, so to speak. Unlike Nick, who's the driven super-achiever, and poor Alex, who doesn't seem capable of a blessed thing, I spend my time having fun.'

He paused to light a cigarette. 'You're not what I expected.'

'Everyone says that,' Anne offered with a rueful smile.

'That's because Nick goes in for blondes, as a general rule, and they're usually very well endowed, like——'

'Like Liv,' Anne supplied when he stopped, looking acutely uncomfortable. 'Don't worry—I know all about her.'

'So I didn't put my foot in it again? That's good—not that you need to worry,' Bill hastened to add. 'Nick's tastes have obviously changed.'

'Which tastes are those?' asked Nick, appearing in the open doorway.

'Your tastes in women, of course,' Bill explained cheerfully. 'I was just telling Anne that she's not your usual type. She's much more subtle, and frankly, I think she makes a pleasant change. It's always surprised me that you went for the obvious and slightly overblown types.'

'Why don't you shut up, Bill?' Nick said pleasantly. 'There's no need to discuss my previous taste in women in front of Anne—no need to discuss it at all, come to that. Things change,' he added absently, coming to stand behind her chair, placing his hands on her shoulders, his fingers lightly stroking the hollow at the base of her throat. 'Don't they, love?'

'I wouldn't know,' she answered tartly. 'I haven't been with you long enough to tell.'

'Feeling insecure, Anne? You should know better.' His fingers moved slowly down to find the valley between her breasts. 'You should know by now that you please me,' he added softly, his lips against her hair.

'Nick,' she protested faintly, painfully aware that Bill was watching this little demonstration with avid interest.

'Sorry, love. I shouldn't make you blush like that.' Nick dropped a careless kiss on her cheek, then sat down in the chair next to hers. 'So, Bill, why are you here?' he asked bluntly.

'To extend an invitation. Our esteemed sister-in-law wants the two of you to have lunch with her.'

'I think not,' Nick said coolly. 'I promised Anne that I'd take her into town for lunch. Didn't I, love?' he asked, his eyes holding hers.

'And to see the shops,' she improvised quickly, 'but I suppose it can wait.' She shrugged, attempting a pout.

'No, it can't.' He smiled his approval for her alone. 'Since I've neglected you most of the morning, it's the least I can do. Tell Liv we send our regrets,' he told Bill carelessly, 'and that we'll see her at dinner.'

'She won't be pleased,' Bill warned.

'But Liv's feelings don't matter to me as much as Anne's. You may tell her that,' Nick finished, making it clear to Bill that he was dismissed. 'Thank you, love,' he said to Anne, when they were alone again. 'If you continue to follow my lead as well as you just did, we shouldn't have any problems. Now, are you ready to leave?'

'Are we really going? I thought it was just a polite fiction.'

'Call it a happy inspiration,' he suggested drily, 'but there's no reason why we shouldn't have a bit of fun. We'll have lunch and see the shops, and if I'm very good, perhaps you'll let me buy you something.'

The town was small, with a slow and sleepy picturesque charm. The houses were a pleasant mix of pastel shades, little haphazard structures, with more substantial colonial buildings fronting on the harbour.

'We'll do the shops first,' Nick decided as he parked the jeep, 'but be warned. This is hardly a Mecca for tourists.'

'It looks more like a Mecca for serious drinkers,' Anne observed, noting the numbers of little stores doubling as bars.

'The locals gather in those places to socialise in the evening,' he explained as he took her arm to guide her around a knot of people in the narrow street. 'Besides, rum is cheap.'

'It must be,' Anne agreed light-heartedly, smiling up at him, thinking how much more approachable he seemed in jeans and a casual jersey, dark glasses with aviator frames hiding his cool grey eyes. Because she was

YOU COULD WIN THE
MILLION DOLLAR
GRAND PRIZE
IN *Harlequin's*
BIGGEST SWEEPSTAKES

6 GAME TICKETS INSIDE!
ENTER TODAY!

IT'S FUN! IT'S FREE!
AND IT COULD MAKE YOU A
MILLIONAIRE

If you've ever played scratch-off lottery tickets, you should be familiar with how our games work. On each of the first four tickets (numbered 1 to 4 in the upper right) there are Pink Metallic Strips to scratch off.

Using a coin do just that—carefully scratch the PINK strips to reveal how much each ticket could be worth if it is a winning ticket. Tickets could be worth from $10.00 to $1,000,000.00 in lifetime money.

Note, also, that each of your 4 tickets has a unique sweepstakes Lucky Number…and that's 4 chances for a **BIG WIN!**

FREE BOOKS!

At the same time you play your tickets for big prizes, you are invited to play ticket #5 for the chance to get one or more free book(s) from Harlequin. We give away free book(s) to introduce readers to the benefits of the Harlequin Reader Service®.

Accepting the free book(s) places you under no obligation to buy anything! You may keep your free book(s) and return the accompanying statement marked "cancel." But if we don't hear from you, then every month we'll deliver 6 of the newest Harlequin Presents® novels right to your door. You'll pay the low subscriber price of just $2.24* each—a saving of 26¢ apiece off the cover price! And there's *no* charge for shipping and handling!

Of course, you may play "THE BIG WIN" without requesting any free book(s) by scratching tickets #1 through #4 only. But remember, that first shipment of one or more books is FREE!

PLUS A FREE GIFT!

One more thing, when you accept the free book(s) on ticket #5, you are also entitled to play ticket #6, which is GOOD FOR A GREAT GIFT! Like the book(s), this gift is totally free and yours to keep as thanks for giving our Reader Service a try!

So scratch off the PINK STRIPS on all your BIG WIN tickets and send for everything today! You've got nothing to lose and everything to gain!

THE BIG WIN

Here are your BIG WIN Game Tickets, worth from $10.00 to $1,000,000.00 each. Scratch off the PINK METALLIC STRIP on each of your Sweepstakes tickets to see what you could win and mail your entry right away. (SEE OFFICIAL RULES IN BACK OF BOOK FOR DETAILS!)

This could be your lucky day – GOOD LUCK!

1 Scratch PINK METALLIC STRIP to reveal potential value of this ticket if it is a winning ticket. Return all game tickets intact.

THE BIG WIN — LUCKY NUMBER

1N 134184

2 Scratch PINK METALLIC STRIP to reveal potential value of this ticket if it is a winning ticket. Return all game tickets intact.

THE BIG WIN — LUCKY NUMBER

3G 131787

3 Scratch PINK METALLIC STRIP to reveal potential value of this ticket if it is a winning ticket. Return all game tickets intact.

THE BIG WIN — LUCKY NUMBER

9I 067404

4 Scratch PINK METALLIC STRIP to reveal potential value of this ticket if it is a winning ticket. Return all game tickets intact.

THE BIG WIN — LUCKY NUMBER

5S 064366

5 We're giving away brand new books to selected individuals. Scratch PINK METALLIC STRIP for number of free books you will receive.

FREE BOOKS — AUTHORIZATION CODE

130107-742

6 We have an outstanding added gift for you if you are accepting our free books. Scratch PINK METALLIC STRIP to reveal gift.

FREE GIFT — AUTHORIZATION CODE

130107-742

YES! Enter my Lucky Numbers in THE BIG WIN Sweepstakes and when winners are selected tell me if I've won any prize. If PINK METALLIC STRIP is scratched off on ticket #5, I will also receive one or more FREE Harlequin Presents® novels along with the FREE GIFT on ticket #6, as explained on the opposite page.

(U-H-P-01/91) 106 CIH ACEC

NAME _____

ADDRESS _____ APT. _____

CITY _____ STATE _____ ZIP _____

Offer limited to one per household and not valid to current Harlequin Presents® subscribers.
© 1991 HARLEQUIN ENTERPRISES LIMITED.   PRINTED IN U.S.A.

*Carefully
detach card
along dotted
lines and
mail today!
Play
all your
BIG WIN
tickets
and get
everything
you're
entitled to—
including
FREE BOOKS
and a
FREE GIFT!*

NO POSTAGE
NECESSARY
IF MAILED
IN THE
UNITED STATES

BUSINESS REPLY MAIL
FIRST CLASS MAIL   PERMIT NO. 717   BUFFALO, NY

POSTAGE WILL BE PAID BY ADDRESSEE

HARLEQUIN READER SERVICE
THE BIG WIN SWEEPSTAKES

3010 Walden Ave.
P.O. Box 1867
Buffalo, NY 14240-9952

suddenly liking him so much, she was gracious in accepting the wild floral print caftan and the pretty necklace of shells he chose for her in one of the small shops near the harbour.

A little further on was a ramshackle building with a few tables at the side. 'It doesn't look like much,' Nick told her, 'but they serve the best grilled fish on the island here.'

'If you say so,' she agreed doubtfully, letting him order for her. She sipped a rum punch and nibbled on coconut chips until their meal was served, and then the aroma of the fish made a believer of her.

'How did you meet Joel?' he asked after their waiter had departed.

'He came into the gallery where I was working,' she explained between bites. 'I'd been in New York for over a year, taking art lessons and working there. When Joel came in that first day, we just started talking and didn't stop, and when I finished work he took me out for a meal. We just *liked* each other,' she continued doggedly, wondering if Nick—if anyone—could possibly understand the magic of finding Joel. 'We saw each other every day for a week, and then he asked me to come and live with him. I couldn't believe it when he asked me, and it was so good to have someone care about me and think I was special! Right away, he began to turn my life around. He told me I had *possibilities*, and that I shouldn't bother with my painting.'

'I didn't know you were an artist,' said Nick, and because she was looking down at her plate, she missed the sharp curiosity in his eyes. 'Tell me about that.'

'There's nothing to tell, because I'm not—that's just the point,' she contradicted quickly. 'I'd been trying to paint, but he looked at my work and told me that I was wasting my time. There was nothing in my work, you see,' she continued, quoting Joel now. 'It was dull and predictable and not even very well done. There was no point in wasting my time—or his—on what was basically nothing but junk.'

'Those are Joel's words, I suppose.'

'Yes, and you know what an eye he has. His judgement is absolutely faultless!' And his judgement of her had been hard to believe, she remembered. 'Your art isn't important, Annie,' he'd told her, framing her face with his hands, the sheer force of his personality overcoming her doubt and insecurity. '*You* are the important thing! You're an absolute marvel, Annie dear, or at least you will be by the time I'm done with you. God, I can't believe my luck in finding you! Little girl, you're something beyond my wildest dreams!'

'You see,' she explained now to Nick, the memory of that moment still lighting her face, 'Joel had already decided that I had mystery and the makings of something spectacular, so that I could attract people and influence them.'

'That's impressive stuff,' Nick observed mildly, 'but did you really want to attract and influence people?'

'I didn't care, except that I wanted to do what Joel wanted, and he said I could use myself to help him get his gallery that way—by being what he could make me into. He——' She broke off, biting her lip when she saw Nick's sceptical smile. 'Oh, you're going to start being critical of him again, and it's just because you don't understand!'

'I'm trying,' he told her with unexpected gentleness, 'but there's so much of what Joel wants. I never hear what *you* might want.'

'But it's the same thing! I'd do *anything* for Joel!'

'Yes, you proved that pretty convincingly when you took on this job,' he agreed with a disarming smile. 'Tell me, do you still paint at all?'

Anne shrugged. 'I just sketch once in a while, for my own amusement—nothing more.'

'That seems a shame. Surely you enjoyed it, and I don't see why you shouldn't keep it up.'

'Because I'm not very good—which you'd know if you'd ever seen my work. Joel was right—not necessarily about my being beautiful, but about my not being an artist.'

'Are you sure?' Nick asked, and she heard a hint of scepticism in his voice.

'Of course! Joel *knows* about these things. He's got a wonderful eye and impeccable judgement. If he says I'm not an artist, then I'm not!'

'Well, he was right about one thing, at any rate,' Nick observed. 'You are quite extraordinarily lovely, although I don't see that you needed to give up your art because of that.'

'But I've already told you—I didn't look like this until Joel took me in hand.'

'Which he did to use you to promote himself,' Nick put in coolly, getting to his feet and dropping some cash on the table, 'and I suppose you love him so much that you don't mind. But all he really did,' he added casually, taking her arm as they started back to the jeep, 'was gild the lily.'

Of course that wasn't true, Anne reflected during the silent ride back to the cottage. It was nice that Nick thought so, but he hadn't known her before Joel, when she'd been stiff and awkward and always painfully unsure of herself. In fact, if it hadn't been for Joel's success in making her over and giving her confidence in herself, she wouldn't have been able to play this game with Nick. The problem was that she couldn't tell him that. He didn't want to hear how clever Joel was, or how wise and how kind. Nick preferred to think the worst of Joel, so she was forced to nurse her grievance in silence.

'We'll change and go down to the beach now,' Nick announced as they entered the cottage. 'I feel like swimming—in the ocean this time.'

'You go ahead. I'd rather stay here.'

'Sulking, love?' Nick reached for her wrist, imprisoning it in his grasp when she would have gone out on to the veranda. 'What's the matter? Is your nose out of joint because I dared say something critical about your precious Joel?'

'Of course not.' Anne tried to pull away, but he merely tightened his grip, holding her firmly in place. 'I just don't feel like going swimming. I'd like to rest for a while.'

'You can rest on the beach. You managed a nap yesterday.' He forced her into the bedroom. 'I want you with me.'

'Why?' she asked crossly.

'Because it's part of the game, love.' He smiled, releasing her wrist, but only so he could use both hands to catch her by the waist and pull her closer. 'You shouldn't get angry with me,' he said softly, bending his head to hers. 'When you do, you're too damned attractive——'

'Stop it, Nick!'

'—and you make it hard for me to stick to my part of the game plan,' he continued, his lips just inches from her own. 'You see, Liv's bound to make contact with me at some point this afternoon, and I need you to serve as chaperon. If you insist, we'll stay here, but all things considered, wouldn't you feel safer on the beach—where you know things can't get completely out of control?'

'Damn you!' He'd left her with no choice; they both knew it, and he smiled as he released her, watching her pick up her bikini and stalk into the bathroom to change.

On the beach, he dropped their towels and the tube of sun-screen on the sand, then caught her hand, compelling her towards the water's edge. 'Come on, love, you'd better swim for a while. You're so mad at me that I'm afraid you'll hit me if you don't take your aggression out on the waves!'

Once in the water, Anne did her best to ignore him, striking out on her own to attack the breaking waves. She knew that he stayed near her, but she refused to look in his direction and they didn't speak until they had left the water and dried themselves.

'Use this,' Nick commanded, handing her the tube of sun-screen.

It made her uncomfortable that he watched the entire process as she applied the lotion; it didn't help that he knew how she was feeling. A smile played at the corners of his mouth and his eyes, narrowed against the sun, showed his amusement. But only that, she noted sourly. There was no hunger in his eyes when he watched *her*; he saved that emotion for Liv—and she wasn't Liv, Anne acknowledged unhappily. Joel might think she had mystery, but that was nothing compared to Liv's incredible beauty and blatant sexuality. No one—least of all Nick!—would ever look at her the way he'd looked at Liv; unaccountably, that thought depressed her.

'I'll do your back,' he told her when she was done, and she pointedly turned away from him, biting her lip when she felt his hands begin their work.

She could just imagine what he would make of this process if he were doing it to Liv, she thought as he worked slowly up and down her back. Today, he hadn't even bothered to release the ties of her top, and there was nothing—*nothing!*—about his touch to which she could take even the slightest exception. Which ought to please her, she conceded, but she was in such a bad mood now that she doubted anything could please her.

'Now you do mine,' ordered Nick.

'Yours doesn't need doing,' she objected crossly, turning back to him when he handed the sun-screen to her. 'You're too brown to burn.'

'Do it anyway,' he said, stretching out to his full length on one of the towels. 'Think of our audience.'

'That's always your answer,' she snapped. Then he shifted slightly, to pillow his head on his arms, and her gaze was drawn to the sensuous play of muscles beneath the smooth brown skin. Her mouth was suddenly dry, she discovered, her heart beating faster as she fumbled with the tube. 'Haven't people got anything better to do than watch us?'

'I doubt it,' he told her, his voice a detached and lazy drawl. 'Anne,' he prompted after a moment's silence, 'I'm waiting.'

'And I'm expected to perform,' she said bitterly, starting to smooth on the lotion. Beneath her hands, she could feel his powerfully muscled strength; against her will, she began to trace the breadth of his shoulders, learning the spare economy of his lean, hard grace. 'You enjoy putting me in this position, don't you?'

'It amuses me.'

Of course it did! Anne thought viciously, only half aware that her hands were now exploring further. Everything about her amused him; *she* amused him, but Liv did not! It amused him to maintain his iron self-control while she lost hers, Anne brooded. *He* saved his loss of self-control for Liv—and she was sick to death of it, of *everything*! Suddenly, her emotions a tangle of confusion, she wanted to shake him, to make him feel the way he always made her feel, to pay him back for all those times. . .to pay him back for wanting Liv. . . Damn him! she thought, her hands kneading slowly down to the point where smooth brown skin met the band of his swimming trunks.

'Everything I do amuses you.'

'That's right,' he agreed slowly, his voice blurring slightly, 'and you do it all so well.'

'I have to—to make sure you get your money's worth.' With a daring she hadn't known she possessed, she leaned closer, until her hands could probe the flat planes of his stomach.

'You're doing that,' he murmured, and when she started to withdraw her hands he turned and caught them with his own. 'Lord, don't stop now!'

'I suppose I'm still performing for our audience,' she teased, now thoroughly caught up in the game, hearing, as his breathing quickened, her effect on him. Deliberately, she freed one hand, resting it on his shoulder to steady herself as she lay down beside him. 'Do you think they're enjoying this?'

'Not as much as I am.' He drew a sharp breath as her hand moved lightly on his chest. 'Yes. . .that's right. . .'

'What are you doing, Nick?' she asked, her body turning willingly into the line of his when he drew her to him. 'Are you thinking of Liv?'

'Forget about Liv,' he said unevenly, his lips seeking hers. 'She doesn't matter now.'

'Of course she does,' Anne taunted, turning her head away, avoiding his kiss. 'I'm here because she matters! You can play your games with me and keep your cool because she matters—you won't even *look* at another woman because she matters so damn much!'

'Is that what this is all about?' Nick asked softly, laughter in his voice. 'Are you jealous, love?'

'Of course not!'

'But I think you are,' he teased, turning unexpectedly to pin her beneath him, smiling down at her. 'Do you want me to love you, Anne?'

'No! I was only trying——' she faltered when she felt his hand stroking the curve of her hip, moving up to span her waist '—trying to pay you back,' she finished unsteadily.

'You've got a funny way of doing it,' he murmured, his hand still moving higher, until he could finger the fabric stretched tautly across her breasts. 'No, love, I think you wanted this. . .and this,' he added as his lips began to tease at hers.

She was lost, she realised in despair, her thoughts beginning to scatter. She'd carried her game too far, and now. . .now he was winning. . .she was wanting him. 'Please, Nick,' she whispered, pushing ineffectually against his chest. 'I was only trying——'

'You were playing with fire, love,' he told her, one hand capturing both of hers while the other found the ties of her bikini top and began to work to free the knots. 'You should have thought of that before you started.'

'I know,' she began, and then he silenced her with a deep, invasive kiss, driving everything from her mind except the slow spiral of desire. She felt his hand against her breasts, moving slowly and with deliberate care as he brushed the scraps of fabric aside in an erotic exercise that left her weak with longing. Then, releasing her from his kiss, he bent his head as she moved restlessly beneath him. She felt his lips, like fire down the curve of her breast, heard the pounding of her heart. . .and in the distance, someone calling his name.

Without warning, her world shifted alarmingly, Nick swore softly and she went rigid under him. 'Of all the times. . .damn Kitt,' he said unsteadily, still holding her captive as he drew one long deep breath. 'So. . .saved in spite of yourself,' he observed with a strange, unreadable smile, finally shifting his weight from her and retrieving her bikini top. 'Let that be a lesson to you,' he told her, now thoroughly in control of himself again. 'You'd better make yourself decent while I head Kitt off.' Abruptly, he got to his feet, dropping the scrap of fabric into her hand. 'Kitt, don't ever do that again,' she heard him say, his tone cool and amused as he moved away from her. For an instant, she saw Kitt's cheerful, knowing grin, then Nick had him by the arm, turning him in another direction. 'When Anne and I are alone down here, *leave* us that way!'

'Sorry, Nick.' As the two men started towards the cottage, Kitt's words floated back to her. 'I wouldn't have bothered you, but your office said it couldn't wait.'

Thank heaven for that, Anne told herself, tying her bikini top back in place with trembling fingers, then clasping her arms around her knees, staring out at the sea. She was horrified—appalled—at what she'd just done. The whole terrible business had been her fault; she couldn't blame Nick *this* time! Worst of all, though, had been the last few minutes, when she had been completely out of control, totally absorbed by an instinctive blazing hunger. If Kitt hadn't interrupted them, Nick could have made love to her here on the sand, and she would have welcomed that unknown and ultimate act.

What in heaven's name had possessed her? she asked herself, staring out at the brilliant sea. Perhaps she had been, as Nick had suggested, jealous of Liv. That would at least explain why she had started the whole stupid business in the first place, but nothing could explain her feelings at the end. Then, the instincts of a lifetime and her love for Joel had been swept away in a few moments of madness!

God, she hated herself, and she leaned her head against her knees, feeling cold and sick inside. If Joel learned about this, he would never forgive her. All those things he'd said that last day, when he'd been hurt and angry—well, they were true now, or nearly so. 'You're damaged goods now, you little tramp,' he'd said, and—God help her!—she *was* a tramp! The fact that she hadn't become damaged goods was merely a technicality, thanks only to the fact that she and Nick had been interrupted.

Now she had to do something to redeem her betrayal of Joel, and the only way was to change her behaviour! From now on, she *had* to be in control of herself; when Nick touched her, she must remember Joel and keep him uppermost in her thoughts. She had to begin this instant, by going back to the cottage to make it clear to Nick that what had just happened could *never* happen again. First, she would have to apologise for starting the whole sorry business, and promise that she wouldn't make that mistake again. Then, with that much settled between them, she would make it clear that they both had to follow the old rule that there would be nothing physical between them unless others were present. If he wouldn't agree, she'd say to hell with everything—the money, the gallery, Alex and Liv—and *leave!*

Full of resolve, she hurried back to the cottage, then found that her declaration would have to wait. Nick was holed up in his study on the telephone, so she killed time, showering and washing her hair before putting on her least revealing shift. When she was finally done, Nick was obviously still on the telephone, his voice a low murmur from the study. Anne took her sketching materials and went out on to the veranda. The sun was low in the sky, staining the sea with brilliant colour, and she retreated into her work, losing herself in the challenge of trying to capture the sight.

She had nearly finished when Nick asked from the doorway, 'What are you doing?'

'Just doodling.' She hastily flipped the sketchbook closed and got to her feet. 'Nick,' she began, bracing herself for what was bound to be a difficult time, 'we've got to talk about what happened on the beach.'

'Nothing happened on the beach.'

'Well, something almost did! I shouldn't have mentioned Liv's name——'

'Damn right,' he agreed, taking a step towards her.

'I won't make that mistake again,' she promised, edging back. 'And you can't do. . .can't do what you almost did. Not ever again!'

'Why not?' he asked softly, still stalking her.

'Because——' Anne backed into a lounger and lost her balance, would have fallen if he hadn't caught her by the shoulders. 'Because it's not what I want. Please!' she whispered, staring up at him. 'I've never been like that before. I *hated* it, and ——'

'You asked for it, love,' he told her with a knowing smile, hands still on her shoulders. 'You asked for it, and you damn near got what you wanted.'

'No!'

'Yes, Anne,' he contradicted with surprising gentleness, 'and perhaps you've learned just how dangerous it is to play that game. I'm only human, so you'd better not try it again—unless you're absolutely sure that you won't have second thoughts after the fact.'

'I'll *never* do that again!'

'Then there's nothing left to discuss, is there?' Abruptly, he released her, turning away to stare at the setting sun. 'Besides,' he continued after a moment, his voice now without expression, 'it's late enough to begin to get ready for our first gathering of the whole happy family.'

CHAPTER SIX

'I SEE the two lovers managed to tear themselves away from each other,' observed Liv, greeting Nick and Anne with a brilliant smile when they entered the drawing-room. Predictably, she was a vision of loveliness, her curtain of pale gold hair a shimmering contrast to her deep blue-violet gown and the sapphire necklace resting against the golden swell of her breasts. 'They don't seem able to keep their hands off each other,' she explained brightly to Alex and Bill, 'and we'd better be terribly discreet about going down to the beach. Yesterday, I, interrupted them, but they were back there and at it again this afternoon. You wouldn't understand, darling,' she continued to Alex alone, giving the endearment sarcastic emphasis. 'You're the cold fish of the family, but Nick—and you too, Bill—are the hot-blooded ones. . .or so I've been told,' she added with a wicked smile. 'At the moment, Nick's blood must be especially hot, because he obviously has only one thing on his mind.

'Not that I blame him,' she continued brightly, after a servant had brought drinks for everyone. 'I know *exactly* how he feels. You're no use at all in that department, are you—Alex dear?' She favoured him with a meaningless smile before turning back to the others. 'He hasn't been for months—his back, of course—but he may be of some use. . .some time.' She shrugged, bending her head so that her curtain of hair hid her features. 'In the meantime,' she added softly. 'I suppose I must wait.'

In the silence which followed those incredible words, she began to toy with her necklace, the movement of her fingers emphasising the swell of her breasts and the deep cleft between them. Unexpectedly, she looked up, grinning broadly as she saw Nick's gaze fixed on the movement of her fingers. 'What's the matter, Nick?' she asked gaily. 'Have I embarrassed you?'

'I don't think that's possible,' he answered shortly, going to pour himself another drink.

'Fix another for me too,' she called to him. 'You know what I like—at least you always did. . .'

'I'm afraid I've forgotten.'

'Then I'll refresh your memory.' Liv glided across the room to stand beside him, apparently oblivious of everyone else as she made a game of helping Nick pour their drinks.

At dinner, she relegated Anne to the far end of the table, where she was forced to endure a litany of Alex's complaints, punctuated by Janet's sympathetic responses. Across the polished expanse of the table, Liv had seated herself between Nick and Bill, where she concentrated exclusively on Nick, attempting to charm him with an air of reckless energy.

Her hands were constantly in motion, touching him each time she leaned close to whisper in his ear. But in spite of her best efforts he increasingly withdrew into a cold distance of his own, finally forcing her to turn her back on him to direct her attention to Bill. In him, she found a more willing participant for her game, and she ignored the others to play to the admiration in his eyes.

When she wasn't forced to listen to Alex's complaints, Anne found herself constantly watching Liv, fascinated by the aura of evil and danger surrounding the older woman. There was a method to her madness, a determined effort to humiliate her husband and torment Nick. She made no secret of the fact that Alex and his ailments bored her. She craved excitement and the attentions of an attractive man—neither of which Alex could offer. She was also coldly calculating in the way she appeared to be ignoring Nick even while she played to him, using her laughter and her smiles, her lush curves and expressive gestures to remind him of her desirability. His withdrawal clearly amused her—nothing more than that—as though she knew the force of will he was expending in disciplining himself to ignore her. 'I know,' her blue-eyed gaze sometimes seemed to be saying, 'I know how much you want me, no matter how hard you try to deny it. Don't think I'll make this easy for you—and don't think I won't win.'

After dinner, to Anne's relief, some of Liv's friends dropped in for drinks, and the tension eased a little in this larger group. The conversation became more general, and Liv finally abandoned Bill, growing even more animated in the company of several attractive men. For the first time, Alex seemed oblivious of Janet, who hovered beside his chair. Instead, his expressionless gaze followed Liv as she moved among the others like a colourful butterfly.

'So, what do you think of the family?' asked Bill, coming to stand beside Anne when Nick was across the room. 'It's quite a spectacle, isn't it?'

'I think it's depressing,' Anne answered truthfully. 'Poor Alex——'

'Poor Alex is having the time of his life tonight, although you wouldn't know it to look at him. He's got precisely what he wants—a nurse of his own to cosset him to his heart's content. Big brother Alex is finally a happy man,' Bill observed with bitter humour, 'even happier to see Liv so thoroughly ignoring old Nick.'

'But she's not ignoring the other men, is she?' Anne asked disapprovingly, watching Liv lean close to one of the new arrivals, smiling into his eyes. 'I don't see how Alex can bear it!'

'But he knew from the start that he'd made a devil's bargain. He was never under any illusions about her, but that was the price he had to pay.'

'Because he loved her so much?'

'Not very likely!' Bill seemed to find the suggestion vastly amusing. 'I don't think Alex is capable of loving anyone but himself. No, what Alex wanted—what Liv gave him—was a feeling of accomplishment, the knowledge that he'd finally taken a round from Nick.'

'What do you mean?' Anne queried.

'You'd better ask Nick,' Bill advised with a grin, clearly enjoying her confusion. 'Perhaps you don't know as much as you thought you did about him and Liv.' He strolled off, leaving Anne standing alone.

Instinctively, her gaze sought Nick, found him standing alone on the other side of the room with a drink in his hand. Although his expression was unreadable, Anne knew he was watching Liv—not that it proved anything, she told herself. Every man in the room was watching Liv; what man wouldn't watch such an incredibly beautiful woman? But did the others watch Liv as Nick did? Anne wondered as Liv's body pressed lightly against that of the man next to her. Briefly, Nick's impassive mask slipped, and Anne saw his gaze devouring Liv with a desire so powerful that it transmitted itself as raw hunger.

It was the same hunger she had seen in his expression when Liv had joined them on the beach, the same expression she had seen when she had taunted him about Liv today. Anne didn't need Bill's cryptic remarks to know that there was more to how Nick felt about Liv than attraction or simple physical desire.

It was as though Liv had some kind of hold on him, Anne realised, suddenly seeing all the small signs she had ignored before. Nick had been intensely aware of Liv all evening—when she had been trying to flirt with him when she had been ignoring him. Even when he had been with Anne, maintaining the illusion that they were lovers, he'd been watching Liv. Now Anne could see, with a completely irrational sense of betrayal, that what she had assumed were withdrawal and detachment were actually nothing more than a total preoccupation with Liv.

Or perhaps the beginnings of self-induced oblivion, Anne decided when she saw Nick pour himself another drink, and realised just how much drink he was consuming. At other parties, he'd been a man of fastidious moderation, but tonight he was drinking steadily. There had been several straight whiskies before dinner, and a great deal of wine during the meal he had hardly touched. Now, while Liv performed for an admiring audience and the evening dragged interminably, there was always a glass in his hand, one he frequently refilled.

Anne suspected that he was trying to achieve an anaesthetising degree of numbness, although—except for a certain careful precision when he spoke, and perhaps an even greater degree of detachment—he didn't appear drunk. After that one revealing glimpse of his hunger for Liv, his impassive mask remained firmly in place. Even when Liv made one last and blatant attempt to force a reaction from him, he showed no emotion.

It came when he finally decided to leave the party, while he was guiding Anne towards the door. Liv broke off her conversation to stop him, her hand on his arm as she gave him one of her devastating smiles.

'Don't tell me you're leaving!' she pouted prettily. 'The party's finally starting to be fun, and you can't leave now, darling.'

'Watch me,' he said briefly. 'I'm doing it now.'

'No, not when Alex has finally gone to bed,' she coaxed, totally ignoring Anne as she dropped her voice to a seductive whisper. 'There's no need to be careful now, and we can do as we please.'

'I'm sure you will,' he agreed without expression, 'but Anne and I can think of other ways to please ourselves.'

'Really?' she asked softly, the full force of her blue eyes turned to him. 'Will she *really* please you, Nick? She's such a grave little thing, and you always liked to have *fun* in bed—or so I'm told,' she added with the now familiar clever, knowing smile.

'That, my dear, is a comment that deserves no response,' Nick told her with his careful detachment. 'Goodnight, Liv.'

After that, he said nothing at all. The soft tropical night was alive with small sounds—the steady murmur of the surf, the song of crickets, the gentle rustle of a breeze among the tress—but he and Anne walked back to his cottage in silence. Once inside, he went immediately to the drink cabinet in the living-room, pouring himself a whisky.

Anne wavered indecisively, watching while he drained the glass and poured another before even bothering to take off his jacket or loosen his tie. 'I'm going to bed,' she announced, but he didn't even bother to reply.

Later, in the shadowy bedroom, she lay in Nick's enormous bed, wide awake. Some trick of acoustics carried clearly even the slightest sound from the living-room, and she listened to his footsteps as he paced the room, occasionally pouring himself another drink or striking a match to light a cigarette.

He was a *fool*, she thought, suddenly furious with him. He was trying—probably successfully—to drink himself into a stupor, trying to forget the woman who was married to his brother, a dangerous, evil woman who didn't care who got hurt while she amused herself. It was madness! Was he going to spend the rest of his life caught up in this obsession? It was a terrible, criminal waste, Anne told herself, wondering why she should care. After all he'd done to her—the petty cruelties, the humiliations, the constant criticism of Joel—what did she care about Nicholas Thayer?

But she did, and she was suddenly driven to go out and confront him. She had to do something—*anything*!—to break Liv's hold on him. She threw back the sheet and got out of bed, pausing in the doorway for a moment to watch as he began to pour another drink.

'Nick,' she said clearly, startling him, so that a little whisky spilled over the rim of his glass, 'what do you think you're doing?'

'Getting very drunk.'

'You already are.' She advanced into the room. 'There's no need to keep at it.'

'But there is,' he explained, and now, in spite of his best efforts, his words were beginning to slur. 'You see, I'm drunk, but not *very* drunk. Not as drunk as I intend to be.'

'Why?' she demanded. 'So that you can forget that you're obsessed with your brother's wife?'

'Ah, so that's what's bothering you.' Carefully, he set down the decanter and turned to face her. 'Jealous, Anne?'

'Of course not! It's just that you ought to have more sense. You're a *fool* to care about her!'

'Lord, I don't care about her. It's that I *want* her.' Wearily he dropped into a chair and closed his eyes. 'You've seen her, you've seen what a marvel she is,' he continued after a moment. 'You can't imagine what it's like,' he finished abruptly, his hands unsteady as he set down his drink.

'You're going to burn yourself up!'

'No. Not with you here, to be my guardian angel.' He looked up at her, vaguely amused. 'You even look like an angel like that—all in white. Although I don't suppose angels wear quite such revealing nightgowns.'

'You'd better go to bed.' Anne spoke firmly, but her words obviously didn't penetrate.

'Liv never looked like an angel—which is strange,' he continued reflectively. 'You'd think that she would— with that pale blonde hair, and those eyes. . . But I was never fooled by that, you know. I knew she didn't love me, but I had her, and I wanted to keep her. And then she met Alex.'

'You can't tell me she *ever* loved Alex,' Anne said fiercely, sitting down in the chair opposite him. 'I don't believe it!'

'No, of course she didn't love Alex, but she made a fatal mistake. Alex was the eldest, and she assumed—I suppose any rational person would—that he had the most money. Instantly, I was out and Alex was in.'

'She married him for his money?'

'For the money she *thought* he had,' he corrected with a bleak, unfocused smile. 'It was, as they say, a whirl-wind courtship, and it wasn't until after they tied the knot that she discovered her mistake.'

'Alex *isn't* richer than you are?' asked Anne, wondering if she'd ever get this infernal family straight.

'Unfortunately not. Grandmother left him what little money she had and the big house, and our father set up a trust fund that produces not much more than Liv's idea of pocket money. I pay the bills, which just gives him another reason to hate me.'

'Of course,' Anne nodded, remembering what he had told her when he'd first asked her to help him. 'That's part of living in your shadow.'

'In his younger brother's shadow,' Nick amended carefully, 'which makes it even harder for him—and even more important that I let him keep Liv.' Abruptly, he drained his glass and got to his feet, swaying slightly as he went to pour another drink. 'Back to the serious business of getting very drunk,' he said, trying to sound amused.

Instead, there was pain in his voice, and, where before she had been angry, Anne suddenly ached for him. So much unhappiness, so much torment, had been hidden under that cool veneer—and would be hidden again in the morning, she knew. Nick wouldn't permit this uncharacteristic lapse to be repeated. If there were any chance of reaching him, it had to be now.

'Nick, why can't you let go?' she asked urgently. 'If you know what kind of person she is, and if you don't love her——'

'But I *want* her,' he cut in with savage intensity. 'When I see her, I'm on fire for her—something you, Ice Princess, will never understand—no more than I can understand why you love that rank opportunist you live with.'

'Leave Joel out of this!'

'Why should I?' he asked with vague belligerence. 'It's much the same thing. We're two of a kind, Anne.'

'I've never been on fire for Joel!'

'Then count yourself lucky. It's hell.' He drained his glass, then set it down on the cabinet with careful precision. 'I think perhaps I've done it,' he muttered, leaning against the cabinet, head bowed. 'Very drunk indeed.'

'Then do to bed,' Anne said firmly, imagining what Winnie would think in the morning, if she came in and found him asleep in the living-room. When he didn't move, she got up and took his arm. 'Nick, you've got to go to bed.'

'Not sure I can. About to pass out, I think.'

'Not here!' She pulled on his arm, forcing him to follow her lead. He was reasonably steady on his feet, but she didn't dare attempt the narrow flight of stairs which led down to the spare bedroom he had been using. 'In here,' she urged, guiding him to the bed she had left to go out and confront him.

Nick sat down heavily on the edge, fumbling ineffectually with his shirt buttons. 'Let me,' she said impatiently, brushing his hand away.

'What are you doing?' he asked as she pulled his shirt off, speaking with the sublime detachment of one only barely conscious. 'Undressing me?'

'Yes.' She knelt to get rid of his shoes and socks. As she straightened up, he fell back against the pillows. Out like a light, she thought, struggling to take off his trousers, out of breath by the time she finally finished the job and pulled the sheet over him. Then she paused, at last permitting herself some emotion as she gently laid her hand against the high plane of his cheek.

She felt a sharp and protective pity as she considered how Liv's seductive beauty and his incredibly tangled family were combining to ruin his life—and Alex's too. Nick was doing his brother no favour by letting him keep Liv. In her determination to get what she wanted, she could destroy them both. Anne thought it was already too late for Alex; he was a weak man, and it was possible that something within him was actually courting destruction.

But Nick was a different matter. He was trying to do the honourable thing, to fight his obsession and distance himself from Liv. And she was going to do everything she possibly could to help him, Anne decided with sudden resolution. What until now had seemed an abstract game to play had suddenly become a crusade. But she couldn't do anything tonight, she told herself, and it was her turn for the spare bedroom. Reluctantly, she started to remove her hand from his cheek, then discovered that he had at least a little consciousness left.

He stirred, speaking her name, turning his cheek into the curve of her hand. 'Can't be alone,' he murmured, and for a moment, his eyes were open and focused on her. 'Don't leave.'

'All right.' Tonight, she couldn't refuse him, so she slipped into the bed beside him, resting her head on his shoulder when he pulled her into his arms.

'Why can't I love you?' he asked indistinctly, but even if she had had an answer, he wouldn't have heard her. He had finally, in an instant, found the oblivion he'd been seeking all evening.

When Anne awoke, it took her a moment to remember why she and Nick were sharing the bed, why she could feel the warmth of his body against her. Her head was still pillowed on his shoulder and he was still asleep; she could tell by his deep, even breathing, by the steady rise and fall of his chest under her hand. She shifted just enough to study his face, struck by the vulnerability she had never seen before.

The familiar planes and angles were more pronounced in the morning light, and there were dark circles under his eyes. His hair lay untidily across his forehead, and she saw that he needed to shave, resisting the urge to run her hand over the rough shadow along the line of his jaw. Even like this, he was still a beautiful man, she thought, smiling at the idea. Not just handsome, she decided, her eyes closing again. He was beautiful in the way she had never realised a man could be.

The next time she awoke, she knew instantly that he was also awake. His breathing had changed, become more cautious and shallow, and his body was tense against hers. When she opened her eyes, she was looking directly into his, could see the clouded confusion there.

'God,' he said, sounding ragged, the tiny muscles around his eyes tightening as he spoke. 'What happened last night?'

'You got very drunk.'

'I know *that*!' He frowned impatiently. 'But why am I here?'

'You didn't want to be alone.'

'Lord, I can't remember. . . Did I do anything?'

'To me, do you mean? No chance of that,' Anne assured him cheerfully, beginning to see the humour in the situation. 'You passed out about ten seconds after you got into bed.'

'Are you sure?'

'Of course I'm sure! Don't worry, Nick. You didn't disgrace yourself or violate me.'

'Thank God for that!'

She felt oddly moved that he so obviously cared, but she attempted to hide that emotion with a joke. 'You needn't sound *quite* so relieved!'

'But I didn't want to drive you away.' His gaze held hers, charging the moment with an unexpected intimacy. 'God knows what I'd do without you,' he added with a ghost of a smile, then winced when he moved enough to put a little distance between them.

No, don't leave me! she protested silently when he broke the closeness between them. She wanted this moment to last, wanted to stay curled into the warmth of his body, her satin nightgown the only barrier between them. She wanted—what she wanted was madness! she told herself. It was time to think of something else. 'Do you have a headache?' she asked.

'Among other things.' Nick turned on to his back, closing his eyes against the glare of sunlight reflecting off the ceiling. 'I feel like hell,' he grumbled, his expression pained. 'I've never been as drunk in my life as I was last night.'

'Would coffee help?'

'I'm not sure anything will really help, but I suppose coffee is a place to start.' He sketched a brief apologetic smile. 'You're being remarkably understanding about all this. I can't think why.'

Because I want to help; because I didn't realise how unhappy you were; because you mean more to me than I knew; because—— 'Neither can I,' she agreed, quickly getting out of bed. 'I'll make the coffee now.'

He was too badly hung over to be thinking clearly, she assured herself when she had reached the relative sanctuary of the kitchen and had started the coffee. He wouldn't have noticed the way she'd bolted from the bed. He'd never know what she'd been thinking, what she was tempted to go on thinking.

Lord! she thought, leaning against the counter, her feelings had undergone a remarkable change in something less than twenty-four hours. Yesterday afternoon no longer seemed real, now that she had seen the vulnerability and pain behind his cool façade.

The fact was that Nicholas Thayer wasn't a happy man, and the reasons why were clearly bound up in both Liv and his bizarre childhood. The discontent she had sensed the night they had met made sense now; she sympathised with him and—remarkably!—was beginning to like him. But that was all, she assured herself. What she had felt for him just before she had got out of bed was a temporary madness—nothing more!

'Hello.' Liv appeared in the open kitchen doorway, taking in Anne's tangled hair, bare feet and clinging satin nightgown. 'How incredibly domestic,' she observed with a condescending smile. 'Nick's making you cook breakfast, is he?'

'Only the coffee. Winnie gets breakfast later.'

'My, you two *are* lazy, aren't you?' Liv advanced into the room, a golden vision in one of her minuscule bikinis, a length of the same fabric wrapped around her hips, sarong fashion. 'Nick never used to sleep this late. In the old days—and I remember *vividly*,' she stressed, 'he used to be up at the crack of dawn, on the telephone to places half-way around the world.'

'Really?' Anne eyed the older woman warily, then instantly decided that there was no reason to be intimidated—or polite. 'Too bad for you,' she added with her own condescending smile.

'Don't be so sure.' Liv's gaze flickered dismissively over Anne's curves, considerably more modest than her own. 'I think we'd better talk. We've got some things in common, after all,' she said carelessly, already turning to leave. 'When Nick's done with you, come up to the big house and find me.'

Yes, your ladyship, Anne said to herself with a smile, then turned to check on the coffee.

'What did Liv want?' asked Nick, cautiously easing himself up in bed when Anne returned with the coffee.

'To talk.' Anne hadn't known whether she should mention Liv's brief visit, forgetting that the house was so open that Nick was bound to have heard Liv's voice, if not her words. 'She told me to come up to the big house when I'm done here. I expect she intends to sound me out or warn me off.'

Nick swore softly. 'I don't want you getting involved with her!'

'I already am. It's part of the game, and I think I ought to make it clear that we're madly in love with each other.'

'That isn't why she wants to see you,' Nick said uncomfortably, staring into his coffee-cup. 'There are things she'll want you to know.'

'Well, if there are,' Anne told him, choosing her words with care, 'I don't believe they'll come as a surprise. You weren't very discreet last night, you know. I've got a pretty good idea why she's so determined to get you—back.'

'What did I do? Tell you the whole dreary story?'

'Enough, anyway. Don't look like that, Nick,' she advised when she saw his dark expression. 'You didn't go into detail, if that's what you're worried about. And I wasn't shocked.'

'Well, you should have been! An innocent like you, dropped into this nest of vipers—I feel as though I'm corrupting a minor.'

'I'm not quite as innocent as that,' she said with a demure smile.

'Damn near.' He studied her face for a moment, then returned her smile. 'Still, you do surprise me, on occasion.'

While he took a shower, Anne dressed quickly, choosing a simple halter sun-dress in a green and orange print. The barriers were coming down, she thought, standing in front of the mirror, brushing her hair, when Nick emerged wearing nothing but a white towelling robe. In New York, they had been very careful about this kind of thing, going to elaborate lengths to preserve each other's privacy. But it was hard to worry about privacy now, she reflected, after they'd spend the night in bed together— no matter how innocently.

'You're wearing that for your talk with Liv?' he asked, studying her reflected image with clinical detachment.

'Don't you approve?'

'It's nice enough, but it's probably the least exciting— least sexy—thing you've got.'

'That's the point.' Anne set down her hairbrush, fingering it idly. 'I can't beat Liv at *her* game.'

'True,' he agreed carelessly, 'but you've got a game of your own, Anne. Different, but at least as interesting— and possibly even more appealing.'

'I don't know about that.' She shrugged self-consciously, then turned to face him with a brilliant smile. 'But I'll do my best to convince her that *you* think so.'

At the big house, a maid told Anne she could find Liv on the back veranda. 'Mr Alex and his nurse have just come down too,' she added, obviously assuming that Anne's visit was a social one. But nothing could be further from the truth, Anne thought, hesitating in the dim and shadowy hallway before going out to face Liv.

She was lying in the sun, her golden body glistening with oil, watching with malicious amusement as Alex and Janet debated the relative merits of sunlight and shade.

'The shade, I think, Janet,' Alex decided at last, a wan and painfully thin figure in shorts and a print silk shirt. 'The sun tires me.'

'Last night tired you,' Janet said gently, settling him on a lounger, deploying pillows to support his back and then his head. 'You stayed much too long.'

'But still missed all the fun,' Liv supplied lazily. 'We danced for hours.'

'We know.' Janet's tone was reproachful. 'The music kept Mr Thayer awake for hours.'

'Poor dear,' mocked Liv. 'Perhaps you should have ear-plugs.'

'I'll have to try something, won't I?' Alex asked bitterly. 'It appears that you can't control this insane need to party all night!' He shifted slightly, indicating to Janet that she should readjust one of the pillows. 'Here's Nick's girl,' he exclaimed as he caught sight of Anne, and she was surprised to see his eyes suddenly bright with what appeared to be suppressed excitement. 'Is Nick with you?'

'No. Making some calls, I'm afraid,' she improvised, advancing into the sun.

'Nick's always making calls, Alex. You ought to know that. He's always working or thinking about work—well, nearly always—which is why he makes so much money.' Liv stretched like a cat and sat up. 'Anne's here to see me. I invited her.'

'Why?' Alex asked sharply, but the excitement was gone from his eyes. 'Why should you want to see her?'

'To talk, of course—darling.' She paused in front of him, making an erotic play of the simple act of wrapping the skirt over her bikini briefs. 'She and I have so much in common. After all, Nick keeps us both, doesn't he?

You too, of course, but you don't like to talk about that. Come on, Anne,' she called over her shoulder as she left the veranda, 'let's go where we can have some privacy.'

She led the way across the lawn, towards a flagstone terrace and cabana overlooking the sea from a spot just off the path to Nick's cottage. Liv paused by a portable bar between two loungers. 'Do you want a drink? No? I didn't think so.' She smiled as she saw the expression on Anne's face. 'I suppose you don't believe in having a drink before noon, and I noticed that you didn't have much last night.' She poured herself a generous gin and tonic, then turned to face Anne. 'Nick did, though—didn't he?'

'Nick was under a strain last night.' Anne knew there was no point in denying it; those clever blue eyes saw everything. 'He was worried about how you'd behave.'

'Was he?' asked Liv, regarding Anne with greater interest. 'I wonder why.'

'You *know* why.'

Liv smiled, arching her eyebrows. 'Not bad, but I think you're bluffing. Obviously you're clever enough to have guessed a few things. Did it start one night in the dark, when the two of you were making love, and he whispered *my* name?'

'Sorry to disappoint you, Liv,' Anne said with what she hoped was a pitying smile, 'but he's never done that. He told me because he wanted me to understand——'

'Understand what?' Liv interrupted to ask viciously. 'Did he want you to understand that he still wants me? Did he explain that after I married his brother, his determination to be honourable didn't last long? Did he tell you about that night three years ago? Did he tell you that he's been afraid to come near me since then?'

What night? Anne wondered unhappily, with an irrational feeling that Nick had betrayed her.

'No, I can see that he didn't tell you about *that*,' said Liv with a triumphant smile. 'He may have told you some of it, but not about that particular night—when he forgot about being honourable, forgot that Alex existed!

You *fool*,' she spat, her eyes glittering with cold sparks. 'You think you can win, but you don't stand a chance! He's only playing with you, trying to make you believe that he's over me. Perhaps he's trying to make himself believe it too, but it won't work.'

'He doesn't love you——'

'Of course he doesn't love me.' The idea seemed to amuse Liv. 'Nor do I love him. It's a *physical* thing—haven't you figured that out? Nick pleases me, and I please him in ways you couldn't dream of. *That's* why he wants me! He's not one for emotions—never was—and I don't ask that of him. He doesn't even have to think, when we're together. He only has to *be*—to enjoy himself and lose himself in me. I'm what you could *never* be for him!

'You're not even a pale imitation of me,' she continued savagely, 'and he wants me—*my* body, *my* smile, *my* hair falling around him when we make love. Those are the things he can't stop wanting!'

'Poor Liv,' said Anne, trying to think about the images Liv had conjured up, surprised that she still sounded so composed, 'you've got a lot to learn. You still think that the physical is all that matters, but I've taught Nick that there's more to life than that.'

'You haven't taught Nick *anything*,' raged Liv, her voice shaking, giving Anne the small satisfaction of knowing that her barb had hit home. 'He doesn't want to be *taught*; he wants to be allowed to *feel*, and I'm in his blood! He's addicted to me, and all your fine talk won't change that!'

'Well, we'll see, won't we?' Anne asked, forcing herself to sound unconcerned. 'Right now, I'd say I had the edge. You're stuck with that poor imitation up there with his nurse, and I've got Nick.'

'Not really,' Liv corrected, poise intact again, raising her voice just enough to be sure that Anne could hear her when she turned and started to walk away. 'You're *temporary*! Nick will be with *me*, when this is done. He won't be able to stay away!'

* * *

'Well, you survived, I see.' Nick was waiting for her, looking considerably more human. 'Was it very unpleasant?'

'Yes,' Anne admitted unhappily. 'I *tried* to make her believe that you'd changed, that there's something special between us, but it didn't work. She knows that you still want her, and she intends to get you back.' Now say something, she silently urged him. Tell me that she's wrong! But Nick said nothing, and she stared down at her hands, overwhelmed by a terrible sense of failure.

The silence lengthened until Anne finally drew a deep breath and looked up to meet his hooded gaze. 'I don't see any point in my staying,' she told him, determined to face what had suddenly become her worst fear. 'You've worked so hard to make me believable—the clothes and the jewellery. . .making sure that I could play the game reasonably well. But Liv doesn't believe it. . . It isn't going to work, so I might as well leave. You don't have to pay me,' she added, a scrupulous afterthought.

'For God's sake, Anne, don't be so noble,' snapped Nick, then continued more calmly, 'You really have to stay, you know. Liv may not believe our act, but we can still convince Alex. Besides,' he continued, favouring her with a lazy smile as he placed his hands on her shoulders, 'you're my protection, love. Liv can't get into my bed so long as she knows I share it with you.'

'Which you don't!'

'But she doesn't know that, and we'll see that she doesn't find out. You realise, of course, that if you left she'd be here like a shot, and—given the fact that there aren't any doors on this place—there's no way I could lock her out. No, we've got to make sure Liv thinks we share a bed—for Alex's sake. In spite of everything, he *is* my brother. Of course,' he continued thoughtfully, hands still resting on her shoulders, 'if you're willing, I could.'

'Could what?'

'Share a bed with you.' His hands smoothed slowly

down her back to draw her a little closer. 'In spite of this morning's hangover,' he continued, smiling down at her, 'it was pleasant to wake up with you in my arms.'

Pleasant was all it was to him, she realised, and the knowledge hurt because, for her, it had been something different, something more than just merely pleasant. She remembered that brief moment when she had been awake to see the vulnerability and beauty in his sleeping face. Pleasant couldn't describe how she'd felt then; nor could it describe how she had felt later, when he'd broken the closeness between them. Then, her reaction had been out of character, even a little crazy, but pleasant? Never a word as tepid and bloodless as pleasant!

'What do you say, love?' he prompted. 'Shall we make it real?'

'No!' Anne stared up at him, stiff with resentment. How dared he think she'd make real something that was merely pleasant for him? Especially when, she admitted unhappily, for her its meaning was disturbingly deep! 'That would be breaking the rules.'

'Then we'll change the rules,' he coaxed, compelling her closer, distracting her with the warmth of his touch. 'Why not, Anne?'

'I—I don't know,' she stammered, her resistance melting when she saw the sudden blaze of desire in his eyes. It's only chemistry, she tried to tell herself, but that didn't ring true. It might be simple chemistry to him, but would she be so tempted to give up the fight if all she felt was chemistry? 'No,' she managed weakly, her body already beginning to betray her, moulding itself into the hard lines of his. 'I—I don't think we should.'

'But we should, love,' he murmured, his voice thickening, his lips beginning to seek hers when he heard her small sigh. 'Please, love. . .can't you tell? I want you. . .need someone right now.'

'You want Liv!' Damn! That was the ultimate insult—the worst he could do to her—and the pain cut through the spell he had been weaving, giving her the strength to pull herself free. Moving back a pace, gathering the shattered remnants of her pride, Anne said coldly, 'For your information, I am *not* interested in being a poor substitute!'

'And you would be a substitute, I suppose,' he admitted reluctantly, 'although not a poor one. Don't sell yourself short, Anne,' he told her, smiling again, a curiously gentle smile which had nothing to do with seduction, one which might possibly have been affection. 'You don't need to be any man's subsitute.'

'Except yours,' she snapped, unable to completely hide the pain tearing her apart.

'I'm afraid so,' he acknowledged, and she at least had the consolation of seeing genuine regret in his eyes. 'And don't bother telling me that I'm a fool. I already know it. . . Please, Anne,' he began again, uncertainty colouring his voice, 'can we still be friends? Can we forget this ever happened?'

'I suppose so,' she allowed grudgingly, knowing she had no choice—*wanted* no choice! 'So long as this *never* happens again!'

'Scout's honour,' he promised with a wry expression. 'It's the least I can do, after the mess I just made of things.'

CHAPTER SEVEN

NICK was as good as his word; during the days that followed, he was a perfect gentleman when he and Anne were alone together. Not that they were alone very often, Anne reflected as she began to see just how much time he devoted to his business. A number of hours each day were consumed studying the business reports transmitted to him through the telex in his study or handling the seemingly endless stream of telephone calls which came in at unpredictable times.

'Sorry, love,' he apologised, coming to join her on the veranda late one afternoon after a particularly long session in his study. 'Are you feeling neglected?'

'You know better than that,' she responded drily, and was rewarded with his grin.

'You're not much good for a man's ego,' he grumbled, stretching broadly while Anne covertly studied the play of muscles beneath the rich golden brown of his tan. 'Lord, I'm tired,' he added, casting himself down on the lounger drawn up next to hers.

'When this is over, you'll be ready for a real vacation.'

'This is as close as I ever come to a real vacation,' he explained matter-of-factly. 'There's always something that needs my attention. The company buys up other businesses, ones which aren't doing well through mismanagement or inefficiency—whatever. Then I send in a team, people with the skills to correct what's wrong. Usually—not always, mind you—the attempt is successful.'

It would be, she thought, irony tinged with admiration. Given the kind of man Nick was, she supposed that nearly everything he tried to do succeeded. It sounded like the perfect job for him: fixing companies in the same way he kept trying to correct what he saw as the problems in her life. Still, it was interesting to learn something about what he did—how he made enough money to be so incredibly generous to her and Joel—and she wanted to hear more. 'Then what?' she asked, sitting up and turning towards him, her chin propped on one hand as she frankly studied his face. 'What do you do when you get a company back on its feet, or fail in the attempt?'

'Sell, in either case. When I fail, I cut my losses as quickly as possible,' he explained dispassionately, very much the cold, hard businessman she had once thought was all there was to him. 'When I'm successful, I sell at a good profit, which gives me the capital I need for other acquisitions. That's what keeps me so busy—the constant turnover. It's never a case of getting things straightened out so that I can just coast until the next problem comes along. It's my job to go looking for problems to correct.' He shrugged, favouring her with a rueful smile. 'It never ends.'

'Don't you mind?' she asked.

'I never give it a thought,' he told her, looking genuinely surprised that she should even suggest otherwise. 'It's what I'm supposed to do, what I've always done. My father made it clear from the start that I'd take over from him.'

'That still doesn't explain why you work *so* hard.'

'Force of habit,' he answered promptly. 'Things weren't going very well when Father died. He'd overextended himself very badly, the company had far too much debt, so I was left to pick up the pieces and get things back on track. I had an obligation to make as much money as possible, as quickly as possible.'

'Money, again,' she observed with distaste. 'Money's *too* important to you!'

'And it isn't to you, I suppose?' Nick enquired silkily, turning his head so that his gaze could capture hers. 'Aren't you going to rather extreme lengths for money?'

'But that's for Joel,' she put in quickly. 'Money's *not* important to me, and this is the first time in my life that

I've cared about having more than what I needed for the bare necessities. But you—it sounds as though you've spent your whole adult life *consumed* by the idea of making money!'

'Lucky for you that I have,' he observed coolly, turning his head away, giving her only his unrevealing profile. 'Besides, my adult life, as you put it, started when my father died. There were people depending on me, and on my ability to make as much money as possible—and fast. There were the firm's employees, of course, none of whom wanted to be out of work, and there was the family. My grandmother was still alive then, and she had expensive tastes——'

'And of course you owed her so much,' Anne interjected with bitter irony, 'for all she'd done for you.'

'—and so did Alex and Bill, come to that,' Nick continued, ignoring her little outburst. 'I wasn't going to keep anyone in the style my father had, if I didn't give all my time to the business—and to making money.'

'It might have been better for Alex and Bill if you hadn't!'

'No,' he countered stubbornly. 'They were my responsibility.'

'And still are, and always will be.'

'I expect you're right,' he agreed without emotion, 'but that doesn't bother me.'

'You wouldn't have to work so hard if you weren't supporting them.'

'But now the work's built into me,' he explained, closing his eyes, clearly determined to be done with the subject. 'I started when I was just out of school, and now I don't know any other way.'

Anne nodded thoughtfully. 'So that explains Liv.'

'What do you mean?' he asked, opening his eyes again, turning to look at her.

'Well, I've never understood her attraction—aside from the obvious, of course,' she added hastily, seeing his sceptical expression, 'but you must have wanted the mindless pleasure that's the only thing she could possibly have offered. She said you didn't even have to think when you were with her, and that must have appealed to you.'

'Yes. . .it did,' he agreed after a moment, eyes far away, 'but it doesn't seem to be working now. . .'

'Now that she's making things so difficult for you,' Anne put in sagely.

'So you noticed that, did you?'

'I'd have to be blind not to,' she answered shortly, and caught his appreciative grin. She didn't think the others—Liv's friends—were aware of it, but each evening Anne watched the latest battle in Liv's bizarre campaign.

'Alex sees it too,' said Nick, his expression grim. 'He's there every evening, so frail and painfully thin—like a ghost at the party, always on the fringes of the crowd, but he's always watching Liv—or me, making sure that nothing happens between us.'

But it was more than that, Anne suspected. Alex seemed to be conducting a perverse kind of test; he seemed prepared to go to almost diabolical lengths to see if something *would* happen between his wife and his brother. Maintaining the illusion of family unity, he insisted that Nick and Anne always be present, yet he encouraged Liv to fill the house with her friends. There were nearly always guests for dinner, with more people coming in after for the drinking and dancing which went on far into the night. Those parties were occasions of wild and crowded gaiety—confusing enough to permit an unlimited amount of flirtation and even the occasional brief physical encounter—which seemed to be what Alex hoped would happen between Liv and Nick. 'I think he wants to see you in a weak moment,' Anne told Nick now. 'It's as though he wants—even needs—proof that you covet his wife.'

'You make it sound so incredibly biblical,' Nick observed sourly. 'Of course it is, although it will be anything but, if Liv has her way—and it's damn hard to resist her. . .' Eyes hooded, his face set in lines of displeasure, Nick brooded in silence for a few moments. 'The problem is that she's grown more subtle,' he resumed. 'Since I last saw her, she's abandoned the frontal attack. Instead she plays games with me, and that's not easy. . .'

No, not easy at all, Anne agreed silently, thinking that it must be torment for Nick. Simply be being in the same room with him, by talking and laughing and always being in motion, Liv was proving her desirability. Sometimes, after hours of pointedly ignoring him, she would suddenly tell an outrageous joke and smile directly at him, hoping for a reaction. Other times, when she was sure he could hear her, she would say something—some obscure word or phrase which Anne suspected she had used with Nick in the time before she had left him for Alex—and Anne would know when she struck a nerve in Nick. She would watch the muscles tense along the line of his jaw when Liv cut through his careful detachment. Those were the times when Liv would become incredibly seductive, using her voice and her eyes, her hands and her body, to delight and excite some other man—taunting Nick by reminding him of what he was missing.

Only near the end of an evening would she finally touch Nick as she had been touching other men for hours. She would contrive to bring her body into fleeting contact with his, taking just a moment more than absolutely necessary when she brushed past him, letting the curve of her breast graze his arm when she leaned across him to speak to someone else. She never gave him much of herself—never gave him *enough*, Anne could tell—but that was a part of the subtlety Nick had mentioned.

'Do you know,' Nick began a little less grimly, turning to face her, 'the evening would be hell without you. You're such a calm and steadying presence, Anne.' He grinned across at her. 'You're my sanity, love. I'd never realised how depressingly manic Liv's gaiety is, never seen how cruel she can be—to Alex, of course, but also

to you. All those cutting little remarks she directs
at you——'

'But you needn't defend me,' Anne put in quickly.
Each time he did, Liv would look at her, lips tightly
compressed and fury reflected in her eyes. Anne knew
that it was Nick's loyalty to her that Liv couldn't forgive,
but she wasn't angry with Nick for being so loyal. Liv
intended to punish her, and the thought of Liv's anger
directed at her filled her with a vague and unfocused
sense of dread. Liv, she knew by now, existed on the
very edge of control—immoral, unprincipled and diaboli-
cally clever—and Anne didn't like to think about what
she might do to her. Liv knew ways to wound that Anne
couldn't even imagine; waiting to see what the older
woman would do to her was almost as bad as watching
what she did to Nick each evening. 'She only does it to
amuse herself, and to watch your reaction,' she told Nick
now, abandoning any attempt at the truth when she
added, 'and it doesn't bother me in the least.'

'It bothers *me*!' Nick bit out the words with such force
that it caught Anne by surprise. 'I resent it! You're too
good for that, and she's such a bitch about it. I won't
have her *doing* that to you!'

Heavens, he *was* angry Anne reflected, eyeing him
through lowered lashes—angry because he was finally
seeing Liv in a new light? Could it be that, given enough
time, he'd lose his taste for Liv? Was it possible? Anne
asked herself, hope warring with disbelief. 'What's the
matter, Nick?' she asked, finding safety in masking her
wild surge of optimism behind a teasing note. 'Are you
having twinges of gallantry?'

'I suppose I am,' he admitted, sounding as though the
idea surprised him, 'but then you do that to me.' He got
up from his lounger to begin to pace the veranda. 'You're
the kind of woman who makes a man *want* to be gallant.
Besides, she has no right to take out on you what exists
between us.'

But nothing really did exist between the two of them—

or did it? Anne wondered distractedly, her gaze following him. Lord, there was something about the way he moved, such a fascinating and disturbing blend of fluid grace and power only barely held in check. She couldn't get enough of it—of *him*—she realised suddenly. In spite of herself, Nick was beginning to matter to her, and surely, if she felt that way, then *something* existed between them! It was more than caring enough about him to want him to be done with his addiction to Liv, more than liking him, more than friendship. It was all those things, bound up and held together by the power of the physical attraction she might fight against but could not deny.

She was always so quick to blame him for making her feel that insidious attraction, but she couldn't blame him now—not when he was doing absolutely nothing to kindle her response. It wasn't *his* fault that she couldn't stop watching the way hard muscles played beneath his teak-brown skin. He wasn't making her want to feel his touch, to touch him in return. . .'But it's not real,' she told herself, only realising she had spoken the words aloud when Nick turned to look at her. 'Nothing really exists between us,' she continued, needing to remind them both of that reality. 'It's only that Liv *thinks* something does.'

'Which doesn't mean that I'm going to let her get away with insulting you,' he insisted, but Anne's dose of reality must have worked, because his anger had disappeared, replaced by a teasing smile. 'Anyway, I've got to defend you. If I don't, Alex will suspect that things aren't what they seem between us, and it's vital to make him believe he can trust me.'

Anne thought that Alex was beginning to believe it; certainly the two brothers had arrived at a kind of truce. She doubted that they would ever be really close—Alex's jealousy and Nick's guilt were too deeply ingrained to permit that. Still, the two men were spending more time together, and at least at those times when Liv wasn't present Alex seemed less defensive and more relaxed in Nick's company.

Until the time, a few days later, when she and Nick were summoned to have lunch with Alex, Anne had made the assumption that Nick's efforts were responsible for the change. Then without the distractions of one of Liv's crowded parties, Anne realised for the first time that there might be other forces at work on Alex.

When she and Nick arrived, both Liv and Janet were with Alex on the veranda, and at first it seemed that lunch was going to be just as unpleasant as the evenings were.

'Are you sure you can make it on your own—darling?' asked Liv with saccharine sweetness as Alex got up from his lounger to move to the shaded table where five places had been laid. 'Wouldn't you like to have your nurse's shoulder to lean on?'

'No, I'm fine,' Alex answered tonelessly, ignoring Liv's sarcasm, 'although I'll want Janet beside me. And you on my other side, Anne,' he directed as he eased himself into his chair and waited for Janet to complete her unfailing routine of adjusting the pillow at his back. 'This is an opportunity for us to get to know one another better.'

For a while, however, he ignored Anne to watch Nick and Liv, seated on the other side of the table. When Liv's arm first brushed against Nick's, Anne saw the same flash of feverish anticipation in Alex's eyes that she had seen before. Then, when Nick paid no attention to Liv, Alex's eyes grew dull again. He was suddenly listlessly petulant, complaining to Janet about the position of his pillow, the spices in the food, the glare of the sun.

He had actually wanted to see Nick respond to Liv, Anne realised with a sense of shock. Now that Alex could see that Nick wasn't interested, he was disappointed—and taking it out on poor Janet. That didn't seem fair to Anne, not when Janet was so kind and compassionate and clearly concerned about Alex, so she made a point of catching Janet's eye and giving her a small smile of sympathy.

'You think I'm being unfair to Janet, don't you?' Alex asked, intercepting Anne's smile. 'I am, of course, but I have very little patience these days. I've spent so much time being ill——'

'And enjoyed every minute,' Liv interjected with a cold smile.

'—and I'm not regaining my strength as quickly as I'd hoped, and then there's the pain,' Alex recited fretfully, ignoring Liv's interruption. 'But Janet doesn't hold it against me. She understands, thank God.'

'She's *paid* to understand,' snapped Liv.

'Oh, but I'm not—that is, that's not *why* I understand,' Janet blurted out, a hot wave of colour washing over her face. 'I just do!'

'Of course you do, my dear.' Alex patted her hand, looking at Liv in mild surprise as she got to her feet. 'Leaving us, Liv?'

'Yes! I'm going out to find some *amusing* people,' she said viciously. 'I'll leave you and your nurse—and the two lovebirds, of course—to enjoy your poor health.'

'Poor Liv,' Alex sighed when she was gone, but Anne was almost sure that there was a glint of satisfaction in his eyes. 'I'm afraid she isn't very happy at the moment, not that I blame her. She doesn't like illness, and I'm still not making life very interesting for her. I think she's feeling just a bit lonely and left out of things. Janet,' he continued, smiling at his pretty nurse, 'I believe I'll have a little wine—unless you say I can't.'

'I won't tell you not to, but I don't think you should,' she said, now sounding composed and thoroughly professional. 'You'll want your pain medication when you rest, but you mustn't mix it with alcohol.'

'Then I'll skip the pain pills,' Alex decided instantly, smiling at Janet again. 'If my back gives me trouble, perhaps you'll be good enough to give me another of those extraordinarily helpful massages of yours.'

'Of course.' Another quick wave of colour flooded Janet's face as she returned Alex's smile.

It was a brief moment, instantly gone, but Anne had found it revealing. She doubted that Alex and Janet were really aware of what was happening between them, but she was willing to bet that Liv knew—knew and was furious. Liv might not want Alex, but she wouldn't want *him* to leave *her*! In Liv's scheme of things, *she* was the one who did the leaving. Just as she had once left Nick for Alex, now she wanted to leave Alex for Nick—and she wouldn't be pleased if things didn't go her way.

'I don't believe Alex and I have ever talked as much as we have these last few days,' Nick remarked when they were back at the cottage. 'Heaven knows we were never close, and I thought it might be impossible now, given the fact that we haven't seen each other at all for the last few years.'

'For three years,' Anne said without thinking, then decided to pursue the issue which had been nagging at her since her private talk with Liv. 'Wasn't it three years ago that you decided that you had to stay away from her?'

'Lord, I don't remember. Something like that, I suppose.' He stared at her, puzzled. 'What makes you so sure?'

'Because it was three years ago that something happened between you and Liv.'

'So you know about that, do you?' He turned away. 'I suppose that's another of the things I let slip that night I got drunk.'

'No. Liv told me, although she didn't say precisely *what* happened.'

'Why should you care *what* happened?' he demanded, and she didn't need to see his expression to know just how angry he was. 'What happened is none of your business!'

None of her business! He was a great one for trying to shut her out, for erecting walls against her, and she wasn't sure whether she was more angry or hurt. Didn't he realise how important this was, how badly she needed to know just what had happened between him and Liv three years ago? It had been gnawing at her since the moment Liv had said what she had; to let it drop now was impossible! Although she refused to examine too closely why the information mattered so much to her, Anne knew that she had to hear the truth.

'Nick, I think it *is* my business,' she countered, sounding braver than she felt. 'You've made everything about me *your* business, and I don't see why I don't have the same rights. Besides, you're in no position to slap me down like that—not if *what* I think happened actually *did*!'

'If I slept with my brother's wife, you mean,' he supplied bitterly, and when he turned back to her, his face was drawn and pale beneath his tan. 'Well, I didn't, but I can't take any credit for that. Alex came upon us in time. It wasn't very pleasant.'

'I'm sure. Alex *wants* you to want Liv, but he needs to know you can't have her.'

'I know,' Nick agreed wearily, dropping into a chair. 'Liv is his only victory over me, even if it was for all the wrong reasons. It's always mattered to him, although I don't think it matters so much now—thanks to you. Our game seems to be working; I think we're convincing him that I don't want Liv, now that I've got you.'

'I think there's a little more to it than that,' Anne told him, repressing a smile. Trust a man! she thought. A man never saw the obvious, what was happening right before him. 'A lot of it has to do with the fact that Alex doesn't care very much about Liv now. He's got Janet.'

'The nurse?' Nick asked blankly. 'What's she got to do with anything?'

'A lot. Something's going on between Alex and Janet,' Anne explained patiently. 'She's very much in love with him, and while I wouldn't go so far as to say that *he's* in love with her, he certainly feels something—a great deal more than I expect he's ever felt for Liv.'

'That's absurd! Alex worships Liv. He'd never look at another woman.'

'Well, he's looking at Janet—*and* smiling at her and patting her hand. You might say he dotes on her, in an incredibly self-centred way.'

'Of course, but that's only because he's still ill, and he finds her useful. She'll leave when he's finally well.'

'Your brother will never be well,' Anne retorted. 'Liv's right about that. Alex adores being ill, and I think he's beginning to adore Janet too. I wouldn't be surprised if he decided to marry her, which would be a match made in heaven—a hypochondriac and his nurse.'

'Alex would *never* leave Liv!'

'I think he would,' Anne contradicted gently, 'particularly if he's convinced that you don't want her.'

'No, you're wrong.' Stubbornly, Nick shook his head, then picked up the telephone and began to dial— business again, a way to avoid thinking about the unthinkable, Anne brooded bitterly as Nick added emphatically, 'Alex could *never* stop wanting Liv!'

What was *wrong* with the man? she wondered, turning her back on him. He couldn't believe Alex could stop wanting Liv because *he* couldn't stop wanting her! How could someone so smart be so incredibly *stupid*? Liv was a bitch—he'd said so himself, not so very long ago—but that obviously didn't make any difference to him, fool that he was!

Seething, she went into the bedroom, wishing there was a door she could slam, tempted to pick something up and heave it into the pool. *Damn* him! Damn him for still being such a fool, for still wanting Liv, for not even being as smart as poor silly Alex! God! she raged, pacing the room, it didn't bear thinking about—so why *was* she thinking about it? she wondered, the question stopping her dead in her tracks.

She was as big a fool as Nick; she *must* be, to be caring so much about his stupidity! Except—oh, it was all such a tangle!—she *did* feel something for him. How could she not? They'd been living in each other's pockets for what seemed like forever, learning more about each other, becoming friends in an odd way. But still, wasn't she overreacting? If Nick wanted to make a fool of himself, why not let him do it? Why work herself into this kind of rage?

Because he was important to her. Like it or not, he was; there was something about him that drew her to him, involved her, made her lose her objectivity. Even now, alone in the bedroom, she couldn't distance herself from the man. She could still hear his voice as he talked on the telephone—that deep, intimate, slightly teasing, *seductive* voice. Even when he was just talking business, his voice had the power to rob her of all rational thought.

Lord, she thought, that kind of thinking has got to stop. It's not healthy; it's unwise and pointless, and I've got to get away from him now—put some distance between us, at least for a while, and be *free*!

Not wasting a minute, she shed her sun-dress in favour of a bikini. Then, armed with a towel and her sketching materials, she slipped silently out of the cottage, feeling absurdly like someone inching away from a great danger. Finally, on the white crescent of sand, the silence broken only by the soft murmur of waves, she was able to forget about Nick and find solace in her work.

'Unexpected, but I like it.'

She had neither seen nor heard Nick coming across the sand. When he spoke from behind her, her pencil leapt, marking her careful work with a harsh jagged line.

'Sorry, I didn't mean to startle you,' he apologised, settling beside her and taking her sketchbook from her hands. The drawing was a simple pencil sketch of dark and ominous clouds over the rolling sea, waves breaking wildly on the sandy beach. 'On such a beautiful day, I wonder why you're drawing a storm.'

'Because.' Anne shrugged to buy time, shocked by the absolute rage she could now see in her sketch, realising that there was no way she was going to tell him about it. 'A steady diet of beautiful days can be a bore,' she improvised quickly.

'I suppose,' he agreed absently, his attention already concentrated on the book in his hands. Before she could stop him, he had flipped to the front and had started turning the pages, inspecting her work.

'Please don't!' She spoke without thinking, her words an instinctive reaction to Joel's scathing rejection of her work. 'Let me have my book back.'

'No.' Nick ignored her hand, shifting just out of range when she reached for the book. 'Indulge me, Anne.'

'But it's embarrassing! I hate to have anyone see what I've done.'

'You shouldn't feel that way,' he told her, slowly turning the pages, pausing to study each sketch. 'You're really very good, with a nice light touch—except, perhaps, when you try to produce a storm at sea.' He glanced up, ignoring her discomfort to favour her with a quick smile. 'Some of these are very good indeed,' he continued, returning to his inspection of the pages. 'This one, for example——' He held out the book just far enough to let her see the page. 'Here you've done a lovely job with the shadows. . .very subtle and deep. And this——' He turned another page, and the two of them stared down at the sketch.

Lord, she'd forgotten that one, Anne realised, studying it as though for the first time. It was the one—the only one—she had done of him, drawn from memory to capture what she'd seen in his sleeping face the morning she had awakened to find him beside her. Now, seeing it again, she couldn't judge its technical merits. Instead, she was shocked at all the precise detail and care she had lavished on the drawing. She'd captured the beauty she'd seen in his face, as well as its vulnerability, and she was afraid she had exposed her own by bringing his to life. To have drawn him so carefully said too much about her preoccupation with him; she felt as naked and exposed as his face in the sketch. He would *know*, she thought unhappily. His eye and his judgement were too good to miss the significance of her drawing. But she was wrong.

'Ah, here's one with a ready-made title,' he said, his

voice shaded with nothing more than detached amusement. 'Sleeping Man with Hangover.' He looked up at her and grinned. 'You weren't very kind to me, Anne.'

'I thought I was,' she managed, relaxing only when he finally turned another page. 'Besides, no one would have seen it if you hadn't insisted on looking. I don't let people see my sketches.'

'You should. You have talent, and Joel is a selfish bastard to have made you stop.'

'It wasn't like that!'

'Of course it was,' he contradicted with surprising force. 'Haven't you been away from him long enough to be able to see what he was doing to you? He was *using* you. You were a puppet until I got you away from him— dressed up in those ridiculous clothes, made to perform for friends and potential backers, not permitted to do something you obviously do very well.'

'But I don't! Joel said——'

'——any number of things to you,' Nick finished for her, 'and none of them makes me like him any better. The irony is that I like him least for forcing you into this agreement of ours.'

'He didn't force me! How could he?' she demanded shrilly, defending Joel with more strength than usual, as though in that way she could atone for the betrayal she could see in her careful sketch of Nick. 'You wouldn't even let me tell him about it, so there was no *way* he could force me to do it!'

'For God's sake, don't lie to yourself—or to me,' Nick objected impatiently. 'Joel had worked damn hard to make you the perfect bait, and he wasn't about to see all that effort go to waste. He'd done his number on you long before I suggested this arrangement, and I can make a pretty good guess as to what he did.'

'You can't! He didn't——'

'He had you programmed, Anne,' Nick continued, ignoring her attempted denial. 'How many times did he tell you to charm me, to be whatever I wanted, *do* whatever I wanted? All that fine talk about how he'd never expect you to exchange your sexual favours for money—I bet *that* went out the window once he'd managed to bring us together.'

'That's not true,' she protested, but her mouth was suddenly dry and, try as she would, her tone lacked conviction. With a chill, she was remembering what Joel *had* said: 'All I want is the money, and how you get it is your business. . .' If only he hadn't said that! It wasn't quite as bad as what Nick was suggesting—or was it? she wondered, feeling a little sick when she remembered that there had been more. Joel had said other things at the same time, but it had all been so vague, so ambiguous, just a joke—the kind of outrageous thing Joel sometimes said but didn't mean. He *hadn't* meant anything by it! She had to believe that, *had* to defend him, had to protect both Joel and herself from Nick's accusations. . .'You're just applying your standards to Joel,' she attacked with fresh energy. 'Just because you'll stop at nothing to get your way, it doesn't mean Joel's the same. He's different and better, and he didn't need to force me to do anything. I *wanted* to do this!'

'You wanted to do it for him, not yourself.'

'Of course I wanted to do it for him! Why do you have to make it sound immoral that I did something for the man I love?'

'Because he's not worth it, and you ought to be thinking of your future, not his. With what I'm paying you, you could——'

'Oh, money,' Anne scoffed. 'I don't need your money—Joel does. I don't even *care* about money. I shouldn't think you would either—not after what Liv did to you!'

'What's Liv got to do with this?' Nick asked sourly.

'You should know better than I. You'd still have her, if she hadn't made the mistake of thinking your brother was the one with all the family money. She's a money-grubbing little tramp, and I'd appreciate it if you'd realise that I'm not a bit like her!'

'I *know* you're not like her,' he said coldly, getting to

his feet with breathtaking grace and towering over her like a bronze giant. 'I was just trying to point out that you could take what you're going to be paid for this business and get established—use your talent,' he paused long enough to hand the sketchbook back to her, 'instead of dancing when Joel pulls the strings.

'You can still do it, you know,' he continued with fierce intensity. 'The money is yours until you give it to him—and he can't force you to do that. *Think* about it, Anne! Don't do anything foolish before you've given yourself a chance to think things through.'

Suddenly he was gone, striding across the sand towards the water, leaving her staring after him in dazed disbelief. They were fighting again, when they hadn't fought in over a week, and it was more than she could bear. She leaned her head on her knees, closing her eyes to hold back the tears which were threatening, wondering if she'd ever felt as confused as she did right now.

What was happening to her? She felt torn apart, and it was all Nick's fault! Because of him, something terrible was happening to her. If she hadn't realised it before, that revealing sketch of Nick was all the proof she needed—that and her reaction to his continuing obsession with Liv.

Obsession—that was what it was, what had happened to her. Nick had become her obsession; this business of being with him was consuming her. He had such a hold on her: that damnable attraction she continued to fight but hadn't yet managed to subdue. Everything with Nick was high drama, a matter of wild and uncontrollable passion. Even their fights, like the one just ended, were conducted on a level of passionate intensity. She fought with Nick in a way she had never fought with anyone else, freely threw herself into their battles with such single-minded determination that she forgot everything but the man.

When they weren't fighting, when they were simply in the same room, it was just as bad. Her need to watch his movements was a compulsion; she couldn't get enough of his lean, hard grace. Simply watching him kindled a strange new response in her that went far beyond whatever it was she had felt at the start of their arrangement. Now her response was far more than a physical one; Nick had become an absorbing passion to her, everything about him a matter of supreme importance. . .

And, because of what Nick had become to her, she was losing sight of Joel! Nick might be passion, but Joel was love. She *loved* Joel—didn't she? Joel was her safety, her anchor, her *life*! How could she have permitted herself to get so caught up in Nick that she forgot about Joel? Oh, it was awful that Joel wasn't still uppermost in her thoughts, in her heart! Something terrible was happening to her, she decided, wretchedly unhappy. Things were going all wrong!

'Still here?' asked Nick, coming back across the sand to tower over her again. 'I thought you were angry enough to leave.'

She should have been, she admitted to herself, and the fact that she hadn't was something else to hold against him. 'I was thinking,' she explained coldly, but her eyes were still drawn to him, absorbing the lean grace of his movements as he towelled himself dry. 'Besides,' she added in a tone of injured dignity when he was done, '*I* wasn't angry. *You* were.'

'Liar!' he grinned as he spread out his towel beside hers and lay down close beside her. 'And I'm not angry with you; I'm angry with Joel for what he's done to you. I'd hate to see you ruin your life over him, love,' he teased, deliberately bringing his leg into contact with hers. 'It would be such a waste. Can you understand that?'

'Of course,' she acknowledged sarcastically, staring resentfully down at him. 'It's exactly how I feel about your obsession with Liv! She doesn't love you——'

'I know. It didn't take me long to figure that out.'

'Then *why*?' she demanded. 'Why do you keep wanting her? It's poisoning your life, and if that's not a waste, I don't know what is! It makes no sense at all.'

'But you're forgetting physical attraction,' he told her with a lazy smile, reaching up to cup her face with his hand. 'If you take that into account, it makes perfect sense.'

'No, it doesn't,' she objected, trying to ignore his touch. 'Physical attraction *never* makes perfect sense!'

'Perhaps you're right,' he agreed carelessly, engrossed in the task of tracing the delicate curve of her cheek, 'but understanding that it exists can go a long way towards making things comprehensible. Your problem, love,' he continued, his clever fingers stroking lightly behind her ear, 'is that you underrate its importance.'

'And you underrate the importance of caring,' Anne countered uneasily, frozen in place even though she knew she ought to move beyond his reach. 'You can't really want—really *love*—someone if there isn't caring.'

'Ah, but caring isn't enough,' he contradicted gently, now threading his fingers through her hair. 'It's not love—not the kind of love I'm talking about—if all you feel is gratitude to the other person for caring about you. That's why I don't believe for a minute that you're really in love with Joel,' he added, his hand coming to rest at her nape, exerting just enough pressure, to bend her towards him.

'But I am,' she insisted, ignoring the conflict between her words and the sudden breathless note in her voice, 'and he loves me.'

'I don't think so.' Slowly, inexorably, with tormenting deliberation, Nick closed the distance between them. 'You and Joel have never done this, have you?'

'I don't think so,' she admitted, lacking the will to resist as he drew her down on to the hard length of his body.

'You know so,' he murmured, his lips already teasing at hers. 'Ah, love,' he breathed, 'has it ever been like this with Joel?'

'No,' she confessed, hearing the one word end in a sigh, hearing his own sharp indrawn breath when she spread her hands out on his chest to feel the play of muscles beneath her touch.

'And it's never been like this,' he told her, his mouth covering hers for an endless, invasive moment. When he had coaxed a response from her, when their kiss was finally at least as much her doing as his, he ended it. 'You see, love?' He studied her flushed and awakened face with a supremely self-confident smile. 'You don't really love Joel—not if I can do this to you.'

Could he be right? Anne wondered, staring at him with dazed disbelief. Each time he touched her, she lost control, but that *couldn't* mean that she didn't love Joel! Joel was her world—wasn't he?—but she'd just betrayed him with her words and her actions, was still betraying him with her thoughts. It had to stop—had to stop now! she told herself firmly, stiffening her resolve, finding refuge in anger. 'Damn you! You keep applying your standards to other people,' she snapped. 'Just because all you can feel for Liv is physical desire, don't think it's the same for Joel and me. He'd *never* treat me the way you do! He respects me.'

'Respect,' Nick repeated derisively, reaching for her again. He caught them both off balance, falling forward with her until she was pinned against the sand by the weight of his body. 'Respect wears damn thin,' he said harshly, one hand moulding the curve of her hip, then moving higher. 'Haven't you ever wondered why there's nothing physical—nothing like *this*—between the two of you?'

'No,' she told him, fighting to retain her self-respect and her pride, fighting to keep herself from being absorbed into Nick once again. 'No!'

'Well, you damn well should,' he told her unevenly, his lips exploring her face while his caressses continued. 'There's always something physical—at least there should be.'

'No,' she said yet again, forcing herself to remain stiff and unresponsive beneath him.

'Ah, yes, love,' he murmured, breathing the words

against her lips. 'If there's none of this between you—and you've already said there isn't—then he doesn't love you. Either that,' he added, his mouth now seeking the curve of her breast, 'or he's not quite a man.'

'Stop it! I won't listen to this!' She raised one hand to strike him, but he easily caught her wrist, imprisoning it in his grip. 'Let me go,' she demanded, her free hand clenching, then digging deep in the sand. 'I mean it,' she warned, and when he didn't release her she flung her handful of sand at his face.

He flinched, dropping her wrist to reel back, giving her the space she needed to twist out from beneath him. By the time she heard him curse, she was already on her feet and running, putting distance between them, heading back towards the cottage.

Once there, she locked herself in the bathroom, taking what seemed like forever to shower and wash her hair, then carefully blowing it dry and dressing before finally summoning the courage to unlock the door and emerge. When she did, she found Nick, still in his bathing trunks, methodically leafing through her sketchbook. She paused in the doorway, warily eyeing his lean and powerful body, his tan even darker in contrast to the pale bedspread.

'So you decided to come out,' he observed, closing the sketchbook and looking up, surprising her with his smile. 'I thought you intended to spend the rest of the day in there.'

'I thought about it,' she admitted, still wary. 'How did you get the sand out of your eyes?'

'Washed it out in the sea, which must come as a disappointment to you. I expect you were hoping you'd blinded me, that I'd spend the rest of my life stumbling and groping. It does amaze me, Anne, that someone with the sensitivity to do this kind of work——' he indicated the sketchbook, then dropped it on the table beside the bed '——can be such a wildcat. You weren't fighting fair, love.'

'I was angry,' she snapped. 'You had no right to do—to try—what you did to me.'

'But you don't always object to that sort of thing,' he reminded her with a lazy smile.

'*That*'s your fault too—along with everything else!' Anne was furious now, glaring at him as she tried to find some way to wound him. Her mind working frantically, she reached for her sketchbook, wondering what she could say to hurt him as much as he had hurt her. Then, as her hand closed over the sketchbook, she thought of the one weapon she knew would pierce his armour. 'I know it's not easy, seeing Liv every day and not being able to touch, but don't take your frustration out on *me*!'

'Lord, you're a fine one to talk about frustration! You don't even know what it is,' Nick laughed, sitting up to face her, seizing her arm in an iron grip. 'Shall I teach you about frustration? God knows, you'll never learn anything about it in that sterile world Joel's built around you.'

'No!' Of course her barb had misfired; she should have known better than even to try firing one, but she hadn't been able to resist. There was something wildly exciting, something free, about fighting with Nick. The prospect of fighting with him always made her heart beat faster, she realised, just as it was now. But Nick always won these battles—that was what she should have remembered—and this one was no different. Her strength and resolve were no match for his as he drew her down beside him on the edge of the bed. What she knew she should fear—what she fought against—she also wanted. Was this the moth and the flame? she wondered even as she made one last effort. 'Nick, no more games!'

'This isn't a game, love,' he told her, transferring his grip and leaning closer, his lips seeking hers.

'Then what? A punishment?' she demanded, fighting him and the conflict raging inside her. She tried to turn her head away, but he tangled his fingers in her hair to hold her firmly in place.

She shouldn't have made this happen and, now that she had, she *couldn't* respond, she vowed fiercely, but it wasn't easy. He was kissing her with a cleverness she had never known before, catching her lower lip with his teeth for a brief moment, tracing the curve of her mouth with his tongue, tormenting her with his feather-light touch. 'No,' she said in weak protest, but they both could feel her resistance beginning to crumble. Suddenly, through the thin material of her sun-dress, she felt her breasts brushing against his bare chest. The sensation assaulted her senses, and a slow spiral of desire began to build within her. 'You can't *do* this!'

'But I can, love. You can't stop me,' he taunted against her lips, 'and very soon now, you won't want me to.' His thumb was stroking the hollow at the base of her throat, finding her fast-beating pulse and lingering there, his long, clever fingers tracing the thin halter strap of her dress, trailing fire down to the swell of her breast. 'Soon, love. . .very soon you'll be wanting what you've never dared want before.'

Perhaps she already did. Certainly, she had never felt like this before; this strange spell Nick was casting was something new—more than she could bear, yet not enough, she thought distractedly. She was confused by the gentleness of the touch of his hand on her breast, the subtle teasing of his lips on hers. He was toying with her, she realised, withholding just enough to drive her mad, waging a leisurely invasion that was impossible to resist. Nor did she want to, she acknowledged, beginning to tumble down the long slope of desire.

'That's right, love,' he told her when her arms crept around his neck. 'Don't fight me any longer.'

'No. . .I can't,' she admitted, leaning her head on his shoulder, pressing her lips to the strong column of his throat, tasting the tang of salt on his skin. How could she fight when he always won? When she wanted him to, she recognised in confusion, when she had always wanted what was happening now.

Surely there was *something* here—something more

than just desire and physical passion—something deeper and stronger, something tender, some kind of caring. There must be! Why else would she want him to much, want his scent and his taste and the feeling that came when she touched him? Why else would he be so gentle, so clever, so careful when he touched her? Why else was he everything to her—everything that she wanted, and more, so much more. Ah, Nick, Nick—the words revolved in her mind until she had no choice but to speak them aloud. 'Nick, please. . .'

'Please what?'

'I don't know,' she whispered as he lowered her on to the bed, leaning over her, a smile playing at the corners of his mouth. 'Please,' she said again, her breath catching when she felt his hand begin to move on her breast, creating an impossible friction against her skin. 'What are you doing to me?'

'Trying to please you,' he murmured, continuing his caresses until she called out his name, gripping his shoulders as her body sought more of his touch. 'Am I pleasing you, love?'

'More than that,' she confessed, moving her hands down his back, absorbed by the play of hard muscles beneath the skin. She had never felt like this before, never felt so alive, so aware. . .so aware of *him*, she realised, feeling dazed. She was caught up in a wild longing to complete this passion between them, her need transcending any physical pleasure she had ever felt before with him. He was her world now, and she craved this closeness, craved its completion—knowing that, without him, she would never be whole. 'Nick, Nick,' she heard herself whisper. 'Oh, Nick, I can't bear it.'

'I know, love. I know, but no more,' he soothed, his caresses becoming gentler as he slowed the pace and began to withdraw, finally calming her until he had extinguished the fire he'd kindled.

Anne tried to resent him for denying them consummation, but her feelings ran too deeply for that. What she had just learned about the fusing of love and desire left her incapable of anything but dazed disbelief. 'I didn't know,' she admitted, drawing a steadying breath when he finally released her. 'Is that what you feel for Liv?'

'Leave her out of this,' he said shortly. 'I wanted *you* to understand,' he explained, standing up and leaning easily against the bureau. 'You don't love Joel unless you can feel *that* for him.'

'How could I?' she asked, refusing to flinch, hiding her hurt as his cold words struck her. 'What just happened. . .it's never been even a possibility with Joel.'

'Yes,' he agreed, regarding her through narrowed eyes, 'and I doubt it will ever happen. Even if it does, he could hurt you very badly. You'd better be careful, Anne.'

'Yes, I can see that now,' she nodded, trying to regain her composure. 'It's a powerful thing. . .'

'Damn right, and don't you forget it!'

'No, I'm not likely to.' He was probably a master, she reflected, staring down at her hands, beginning to suspect that he'd spoiled the future for her. Would she ever want any other man the way she'd wanted—still wanted!—Nick? Would anyone else be clever enough and gentle enough to make her feel as he had? But there was no point in asking those questions, she told herself, feeling empty; she already had the answers. 'Nick?' She looked up, meeting his dark grey gaze. 'Do you think Joel and Thea. . .do they ever make love?'

'Why do you ask?'

'Because I want to know. I've heard rumours, of course, but Joel always said they were lies. . .' But they hadn't been lies, she realised now, biting her lip, remembering things she had never understood, never questioned. There were the times Joel would go out by himself and come back hours later, with Thea in tow. . .the times during the day when he would send her to do a long list of needless errands and she'd come back to find that Thea had just happened to stop by to visit. . .the times when she had come back from an evening with Nick to find both Joel and Thea waiting for her. . . Always, there had been that lazy, comfortable—satisfied!—aura around them. They had always seemed so close, so complete, and Anne had taken that as a sign of the long friendship between them. Now she knew better. They had been feeling what she knew *she'd* be feeling right now—if she and Nick had just made love to each other.

And it hurt! she acknowledged, gripping her hands until the knuckles showed white. It tore her apart—not because Joel had betrayed her, but because his betrayal meant nothing. Joel was the past; he no longer mattered, and the pain came from knowing that he no longer mattered because Nick mattered too much—more than she would ever matter to him!

Now the trick was to make sure that Nick didn't see what she had just learned. She had to hide that—hide *everything*!—from him. 'Of course the rumours aren't true,' she said now, forcing herself to meet Nick's dark brooding gaze. 'After what just happened, I was being fanciful. . .forgetting that Joel would never lie to me.'

'God!' Nick exploded, beginning to pace the room, the magnitude of his anger a tangible presence. 'Won't you ever learn?' he demanded harshly. 'Won't you ever stop thinking of Joel? Can't you see that he's wrong—dead wrong—for you?' He stopped in the open doorway leading to the pool. The silence grew, while he stared out at the water, and when he finally did speak again, his anger was gone, replaced by weariness. 'I wonder if you'll ever learn,' he mused, 'if anything can make you see. . .can keep you from making the mistake of going back to him. . .

'You know,' he resumed after another pause, 'there may be a solution to the problem. We could marry.' He was turned slightly away from her, and his profile told her nothing as he continued, thinking aloud rather than speakaing directly to her. 'It makes a certain amount of sense. It would save you from Joel. It might even save me from Liv. We like each other well enough—at least we do when we're not fighting. We've proved that we can live together without much difficulty. We find enough to talk about, and there's a satisfying degree of chemistry between us. It's no great passion, of course, but that sort of thing only happens once in a lifetime—if at all. I don't see why a marriage between us wouldn't work very well. What do you think?' he asked casually, finally turning to look at her.

'That you're mad!' Anne ignored the new stab of pain caused by his words. 'You don't mean it.'

'You may be right,' he agreed evenly. 'I'm not entirely sure that I do, but it does seem worth considering. Perhaps we should give it some thought.'

'You may, if you like. I'm going for a walk.' She stood up, resisting the urge to slap his face when she saw his appreciative grin.

'That's one of the things I like best about you. When I suggest the most outrageous things—like pretending to be my mistress or actually marrying me—you take it quite calmly.'

If he only knew, she thought miserably, stalking from the room, going down to the beach. He'd just turned her world upside down, shattered all her beliefs, and he thought she was taking it *calmly*! That would have been good for a laugh if she hadn't felt so battered and bruised, so wounded and betrayed. With that damnable attraction of his, he had destroyed whatever illusions she had left about Joel and taught her *too* well what love was. Then, as though that hadn't been enough, he had used his cool and logical self-interest to make a mockery of the knowledge he had given her.

Damn him! she raged silently, kicking off her shoes to walk in the sand. It wasn't what he'd said; it was what he'd *done*. He'd made her fall in love with him, and she wasn't taking it calmly at all!

CHAPTER EIGHT

'LOVERS' quarrel?' Liv enquired brightly when Anne and Nick arrived for dinner that evening. '*I* saw the two of you on the beach this afternoon. It was really quite amusing,' she continued, addressing the room at large. 'Nick was doing the usual—hot-blooded male that he is—when Anne suddenly threw sand in his face. What is it, Nick?' she asked, her tone still light and teasing, but her eyes glittered with a dangerous cold fury when she looked at Anne. 'Is your little girlfriend so sure of herself that she thinks she can get away with anything she pleases?'

'My little girlfriend, as you put it, is special,' Nick countered easily, drawing Anne into the safety of his arms. 'She has every reason to feel sure of herself, and has depths you can't imagine.'

'You're right, I can't,' Liv snapped. 'She's such a dull and quiet little thing—not at all the sort I'd expect you to bother with. I don't think she'll last much longer, not if she thinks she can behave the way she did this afternoon.'

'But you're missing the point, Liv,' Nick explained patiently. 'The spice is part of her attraction. Besides, making up is such fun. Isn't it, love?' he added for Anne alone.

'I——' Anne couldn't answer; she was trapped, paralysed by the venom in Liv's gaze.

'Isn't it, my love?' prompted Nick, turning her to face him, forcing her out of her rigid immobility when he smiled at her.

'Yes.' They *hadn't* made up, of course, but now she returned his smile, holding her breath as his mouth descended on hers. She *needed* his kiss, she acknowledged with fierce intensity, even more frightened of her own reaction than she had been of the hatred in Liv's eyes. She wanted more of Nick, wanted to be closer, to melt into the length of his body—right here, in front of everyone. She was perilously close to revealing herself completely—not to the others, who didn't matter in the least—but, which was impossible, to Nick.

Falling in love was absurd and bizarre, Anne concluded, an inherently irrational act. She had lived with Joel for a year, during which time he'd transformed her from ugly duckling to swan. She had thought she had fallen in love with him; she *ought* to have fallen in love with him! She was grateful for what he had done for her; she was prepared to forget all his small and subtle cruelties, for she could see now that he *had* been cruel. He had bound her to him with a pack of lies and fostered an impossible dependency, manipulated her into doing only what *he* wanted done to serve his purpose. She could understand that now, and she could forgive him— but that was all! The fact was, as Nick had so emphatically demonstrated, that she felt nothing for Joel *but* gratitude and forgiveness.

What she felt for Nick was very different, a tangled skein of emotions—liking, respect, jealousy, desire, physical attraction. . . The list was endless, and an exercise in futility. Unlike Joel, Nick cared about her opinions, was concerned about her future, but the stark reality was that he didn't *love* her! He didn't even *want* her—not in the way he wanted Liv.

All he might offer her, Anne acknowledged miserably, was a marriage that *he* thought made sense. He had talked about liking each other, living together without difficulty, and the chemistry between them. 'Chemistry' was a depressingly clinical and dispassionate word, one which didn't begin to describe how *she* felt when they came together and the fierce, wild longing began to burn within her. 'Chemistry' described how Nick felt about *her*; his wild longing was reserved for Liv, and nothing Anne could do would change that.

What she could do—what she *did* do for the next few

days—was maintain her poise, so that Nick couldn't guess what she felt for him. Not for nothing had people called her 'Cool Anne', and now she used all the skills that—irony of ironies—Joel had taught her.

The only times her poise deserted her were the times when Nick touched her, but that was nothing new. Even before she had realised she loved him, the chemistry he was so fond of talking about had been working on her. Nothing about her response to him had changed, except that now she responded with a greater awareness which was *her* secret.

Only once had she been afraid that he knew what she was trying to hide. It had happened while they were dancing at one of Liv's interminable parties. The music changed to something slow and romantic, and Nick gathered her into his arms, touching his lips to the curve of her shoulder when she instinctively moulded her body into the powerful line of his.

'Lord, you do that so well,' he murmured, lifting his head to study her face with a puzzled frown. 'You're either a consummate actress, or one of the most delightfully responsive women I've ever known. And I don't believe it's an act.'

'I——' But her mind was paralysed with fright—something which seemed to be happening to her with depressing frequency these days—and words failed her. She could only cling desperately to him, dreading the moment when she would learn from his expression that her secret was out.

'And when you blush like that, I *know* you're not acting,' he continued when telltale colour stained her cheeks. 'There's no calculation in the way you react; you're too transparent, too real. You're that rare and exciting blend of passion and spontaneity. Joel was a fool not to see it, but his loss may be my gain.'

'Why?' she asked.

'Because I'm still thinking about marrying you. I hope you're thinking about it too.'

'Well, I'm not,' Anne said shortly, hiding her misery

from him. She knew without thinking that she couldn't possibly marry him under the terms he had outlined, and she knew that he wouldn't change his terms. 'I *couldn't* marry you!'

'No, don't say that yet, Anne. You may change your mind,' he suggested, then kissed her before she could tell him how wrong he was.

Anne was so engrossed in her own emotional struggle that she was oblivious to the changes taking place around her. She didn't begin to realise what had been happening until just before the family gathering was due to end. It was during Liv's last large party, with at least sixty people crowding the spacious rooms of the big house. There had been cocktails and a buffet dinner, and now a calypso band played for dancing. Somehow, in the crowd, Anne had become separated from Nick, and now she stood alone on the far side of the drawing-room, watching Liv.

Tonight, the older woman seemed wilder and more reckless than ever before. Anne could hear it in Liv's laughter, see it in Liv's abandoned movements which caused her hair to swirl around her face in a spun-gold cloud. It showed, too, in her beige gown of fine, gauze-like material which clung to her provocative curves, leaving almost nothing to the imagination. The wanton effect was heightened because the gown was the same honey tan shade as Liv's skin, creating the illusion of soft and floating nakedness.

Most of all, though, Liv's strange mood showed in her eyes. In contrast to the pale colours of her gown and hair, her eyes seemed an even deeper blue, precisely the colour of the dazzling sapphire jewellery she wore. Tonight, her eyes were intensely alive, glittering with barely suppressed excitement as she kept her gaze almost constantly fixed on Nick.

To Anne, it was obvious what Liv intended, what she expected would happen before the night was over. Anne had always known that Liv would stop at nothing to win

Nick back, and everything about her suggested her
conviction that tonight was when she would succeed.
What did it matter? Anne asked herself in an attempt to
be logical. Liv couldn't do any more damage than she
had already done. Nick had belonged to her long before
Anne had appeared on the scene, so what difference
could one night make? All the difference in the world,
Anne admitted with bleak honesty. Now, she knew she
loved him, and it was going to tear her apart to imagine
what was happening during the hours when he would be
with Liv.

On the heels of that thought, Anne saw him across the
room. Her heart lurched alarmingly, the mere sight of
him having an enormous power to move her. Her gaze
fastened hungrily on him, and she remembered the night
she had first seen him, in Joel's loft. Then she had
thought him cold and aloof; she hadn't seen the contrasts
of unhappiness, humour and devastating charm just
beneath the cool façade.

Oh, I love him so! she thought, briefly closing her
eyes against the rush of feeling. When she opened them
again, Liv was with him. They were facing each other,
only a few inches apart, and what alarmed Anne most
was that Liv was performing none of her usual tricks.
She wasn't touching him, there was no seductive smile;
instead, she was speaking intently, while Nick stared
gravely down at her face.

This time, the sight of the two of them frightened
Anne; it was the *way* she was seeing them together. This
time, it wasn't a game. There was something intimate
and very real about the way Liv was speaking and the
way Nick was listening to her. Whatever it was Liv was
saying *mattered* to both of them, and that was what
frightened Anne.

'I wouldn't worry, if I were you,' Alex advised, joining
her, pretty Janet hovering her accustomed few paces
away. 'No matter what happened in the past between
Liv and Nick, it's over now.'

'Yes?' Anne asked inadequately, surprised that he should speak so openly about the subject.

'Yes.' His smile was similar, but less exciting and less alive than any smile Nick had ever given her. 'It's a pity, but poor Liv has every reason to feel left out these days,' he continued, his eyes alive with an expression of cold satisfaction. 'Any fool, even my wife, can see that Nick is very much taken with you. She's lost the game and she knows it. So should you.'

You're wrong! You and I are the fools, Anne longed to say. Instead, she murmured something non-committal, looking back just as Liv turned away from Nick, a radiant smile firmly in place on her face. For a moment or two, Nick's gaze followed her, then he deliberately looked away. Then he caught sight of Anne, smiled briefly and came across the room to join her.

'Sorry, love,' he apologised casually, his hand on her arm in the now familiar gesture of possession. 'I didn't mean to abandon you, but I see you had Alex to keep you company.'

Just as *you* had Liv, she thought with a strange mingling of anger and despair, when he and Alex began to talk.

'Let's go out on the veranda,' Alex suggested. 'Janet, my dear, come with us. I really must sit down and rest, and the air's incredibly heavy in here.'

It wasn't much better on the deserted veranda, Anne decided, waiting while Alex and Janet performed the ritual of deciding which chair would be best for his back. It was humid and the night was very still; there was no hint of a breeze, and the stars were hidden by a dull haze.

'There's a storm coming,' Alex observed when Janet had positioned his pillow and taken the chair next to his. 'I think it will be a bad one.'

In spite of the heat, Anne shivered—another twinge of the fear she had felt when she had watched Nick and Liv together. She resisted the impulse to reach for the reassurance of Nick's hand. Nick could offer no reassurance, she acknowledged bleakly as he and Alex reminisced easily about past storms on the island. What she wanted was the reassurance of knowing Nick loved her, but he didn't love anyone, and what passion he had belonged to Liv.

'. . .of course you weren't here for the worst one,' Alex was saying as a servant came up to their small circle of chairs. 'You were away at school, and I was alone here with Grandmother and the help. I remember—— What is it?' he asked impatiently, finally noticing the servant. 'I don't like to be interrupted!'

'Yes, Mr Alex. I'm sorry,' he apologised, then handed Nick a slip of paper.

'Damn! Pity it couldn't have waited until morning,' Nick said, scanning the message, then pocketing it as he stood up. 'I've got to return a call—business, of course. I'll go down to the cottage to do it. No, love, you stay here,' he told Anne, putting his hands on her shoulders as she started to rise. 'I shouldn't be long. You and Alex can keep each other company again,' he suggested, kissing her briefly before he strode off across the manicured lawn into the darkness.

'You could have gone with him,' Alex said after a moment. 'Nick forgets—no, hasn't *realised*—that I have Janet. She's wonderful company,' he explained smugly, reaching for her small but capable hand. 'Actually, she's more than company. She's become *important* to me.'

'How nice,' exclaimed Anne, mostly to reassure Janet, who suddenly looked embarrassed to death. 'I thought perhaps that was happening.'

'Did you? Nobody else has,' Alex said peevishly, sounding like a child who had been cheated of his chance to tell an important secret. 'Not even Liv knows yet. I'm going to divorce her,' he explained with a mixture of excitement and defiance. 'God knows I've got grounds enough! And Janet and I will be very happy together— won't we, my dear?'

Journey with Harlequin into the past and discover stories of cowboys and captains, pirates and princes in the romantic tradition of Harlequin.

'Oh, yes,' she agreed, gazing at him with a wondering smile, as though she couldn't quite believe her luck.

'How nice,' Anne contributed again.

'Yes, it is, isn't it?' asked Alex, preening slightly. 'I'll be happy now—something I never was with Liv. I should have divorced her long ago—never should have married her in the first place. But there were reasons. . .' He paused, eyes far away, undoubtedly contemplating years spent living in Nick's shadow and further years spent punishing Nick by staying married to Liv. '. . .and Janet and I will have a good life,' he resumed with an obvious effort. 'I'm not sure how much Nick has told you, but it's been difficult. . . Still, it's all ended well. Nick has you, and I have Janet—but don't tell him yet, Anne,' he added urgently. '*I* want to do that myself!'

'Of course,' she agreed automatically, her mind grappling with the implications of Alex's announcement. Still, when he and Janet left her to go upstairs, she managed to wish them every happiness.

They would need more than good wishes, she thought grimly, once they were gone. Janet obviously loved Alex, or at least worshipped him, but love had nothing to do with Alex's decision. He was divorcing Liv to pay her back for the years of humiliating unfaithfulness, and he was giving her up now only because he believed Nick no longer wanted her. In marrying Janet, he was operating on the principle of self-interest—the invalid would have his nurse in constant attendance. The whole business was sick, a perversion of what love and marriage ought to be!

It was also, Anne acknowledged unhappily, much like the kind of marriage Nick had suggested to her, and she was even more determined to refuse him if he brought it up again. But he wouldn't do that, she realised, and the knowledge struck her like a sudden, sharp blow. He wouldn't need to save himself from Liv, wouldn't need to stay away from her once Alex had divorced her. Liv was free now, or would be shortly, and Nick would be able to have what he couldn't stop wanting, could finally let his obsession consume him.

Perhaps he had already gone back to her, Anne thought, standing alone in the midst of the party when she had gone back inside. Liv was nowhere to be found, even though she wasn't the type to retreat to a quiet corner for a private talk. When Liv was present, she was always on display, always the centre of attention. Now it was obvious that she had left her own party, and that could only mean that she had left with someone or to meet someone.

'Where's old Nick?' demanded Bill, confirming Anne's growing suspicion when he materialised out of the crowd, slightly tipsy and wearing a foolish grin. 'Don't tell me he's gone away and left you all alone!'

'He had to make a call—a business emergency, I think.'

'Lord, that was hours ago!' Bill laughed. 'I remember when the servants were looking for him—not long after dinner, and it's nearly midnight now. Do you think he's with someone else—someone who shall remain nameless?' he added, laughing again.

'Of course not!' Had it been *that* long? Anne wondered. 'That's a stupid thing to say!'

'No need to bite my head off, little Anne, and I don't think it's that stupid,' Bill said in mild reproof. 'Liv's on the prowl tonight—hadn't you noticed? There's no need to guess who she's stalking, and the man doesn't exist who can resist her. But there's no harm done, little Anne. I'm here and at your service.' He sketched an unsteady bow. 'Why don't we go up to my room, where we can have some privacy? *There's* a good way to pay old Nick back for leaving you alone!'

'Don't be a fool, Bill. I'm not going to do something like that. I think I'll just go back to the cottage.'

'Are you sure that's a wise idea?' Bill asked carefully, and he suddenly didn't seem at all drunk. 'Look, it might be better if you waited here until he comes to get you. I'll keep you company,' he added kindly. 'No strings attached, no finding privacy in my room. We can just stand here and talk.'

'Thanks anyway, but I think not.' Anne was past the point of holding up her end of a conversation, and she *had* to know the truth. The reality of finding Nick and Liv in his bed *couldn't* be worse than what she was imagining now! 'I'm going to go back.'

'At least let me walk with you,' Bill suggested quickly. 'No harm in that.'

'No, thanks. Don't worry, Bill.' She forced a brilliant smile. 'I'll be fine,' she assured him as she turned away.

Outside, it was even more humid than before, the air so heavy that, once away from the big house, the sounds of the party were muffled and indistinct. The night seemed to have a silent, waiting quality about it. Waiting for what? she wondered—for her to find Liv and Nick in the cottage? She had a quick vision of the two of them in his bed, lying where she lay each night, where she had slept in Nick's arms one night, not so very long ago.

The heavy silence was broken by the clear sound of laughter nearby—Liv's laughter, Anne knew instantly.

'Damn! I can't find my dress,' said Liv, her voice light and breathless in the heavy darkness, followed immediately by the deeper sound of a man laughing. 'It's really not all that funny, darling,' she drawled. 'I dropped it here somewhere, and I can't go back without it! Do you know where it is?'

In the darkness, it took Anne a few moments to realise that the voices were coming from the small terrace where she and Liv had fought their pitched battle. In her mind, she could see it clearly, with the cabana to block the view from the path, an array of chaises—even a bar, she remembered. Nothing could be better suited for what Liv and Nick had obviously been doing!

But she didn't *know* that Liv was with Nick, Anne reminded herself, and suddenly she didn't want to know. As quickly as she could, without making any noise, she began to move past the cabana, heading towards the bend in the path.

'Did you hear something?' Liv asked sharply, and Anne froze. 'No? Good. It would be just our luck to have Alex decide that he'd sleep better for a midnight stroll.'

'Do you really care?' The man didn't sound at all like Nick. This voice was deep and husky—but how was Anne to know what Nick sounded like when he'd just made love? 'It's a little late to be worrying about him now.'

'But we can't burn our bridges—not just yet,' Liv explained gaily, and Anne began to move again. 'Much as I'd *like* to. God, darling, you were fantastic, and you haven't forgotten a thing—even after all these years!'

As Anne heard movement on the flagstones, she hurried towards the bend in the path. Once she passed that point, there would be no danger of being seen. With luck, perhaps even the sound of the voices behind her would be absorbed by the heavy night air! But not yet——

'What are you *doing*?' Liv demanded with a laugh, the sound silvery in the darkness. 'What? Again?' she asked, and Anne could hear the excited anticipation in her voice. 'The hell with my dress! You're impossible—but quite marvellous, darling Nick.'

There were no more words—just the sound of movement and laughter, following Anne until she was far past the bend in the path.

No! she thought. No, no *no*! She couldn't *bear* it! To know what was happening—to know Liv had won, to know that Nick and Liv were doing what he would never do with her!

Ahead, the cottage was nearly dark, only one dim lamp burning to guide her back. Every other night, she had returned to the cottage with Nick, but he wasn't with her now. He was back there with Liv, and they were doing what *she* wanted to do—to share—with Nick. The thought tore her apart. Damn him for being a fool! she thought as she crept silently along the veranda and into the bedroom. Damn him for giving in to Liv in the end, for betraying *her*!

'Damn him!' She said the words aloud, fiercely, to the empty, listening cottage. She was alone here, and from the sound of things back on the terrace, she would be alone for some time—perhaps even for hours, unless it stormed in the meantime. She hoped it would! She hoped the two of them would get drenched—struck by lightning, she added spitefully.

For the time being, she had the cottage to herself, and she could do as she pleased. Briefly, she considered getting drunk, then rejected the idea. That had been Nick's solution, but she wasn't the fool *he* was! Instead she undressed, carelessly dropping everything on the floor—her dress, the silk stockings and lacy lingerie, even the emeralds Nick had given her. Then, obeying a mad impulse born of rebellion and the pain of betrayal, she decided against a sensible shower. 'I shall do as I *please*,' she announced aloud, marching across the room and through the open doorway to dive cleanly into the pool.

She needed something like this, she realised, gasping as the cool water closed over her. 'And Nick can go to *hell*!' she yelled when she came up for air. She *needed* to push herself to her physical limits—something, anything, to drive away or at least blunt the pain she was feeling.

With mechanical, driven precision, she swam countless laps—one end of the pool to the other, turning smoothly to repeat the process, never stopping, never slowing her pace. She was feeling better with every lap, she thought with a sense of exhiliaration, briefly forgetting Nick and Liv and what they were doing together. She swam until fatigue finally caught her, until her legs lost their kick and her arms could no longer cut cleanly through the water, until her breathing came only in short, painful gasps as she tried to draw enough air into her lungs.

Drowning seemed a distinct possibility, she decided

vaguely, forcing herself to swim the distance to the side of the pool. It couldn't have been more than fifteen feet away, but it was almost more than she could manage. When she reached the narrow porch, she gripped the smooth surface with trembling fingers, her body still in the water as she struggled to fill her lungs.

'You're better than I thought,' she heard Nick say, and his strong hands gripped her arms to pull her from the water. 'That was impressive, love, although I wonder why you did it.'

She was hauled unceremoniously on to the deck, and when her legs wouldn't support her, she was forced to endure the humiliation of being held upright. His hands dug painfully into her arms while she leaned weakly against him, still fighting to catch her breath.

'You're back——' she managed, and after the next breath '——sooner than I expected.'

'Back from where?' he asked mildly, moderating his hold when her legs began to show some promise of supporting her. 'Where am I supposed to have been?'

'With Liv.'

'Not on your life!' he laughed shortly. 'I've been here, my ear glued to the telephone. Can you stand on your own yet?'

'Yes, but——'

'Good. I'll get you a towel.'

'But I *heard* you!' Anne called after him, leaning against the doorframe, trying not to drip on the bedroom floor. She didn't believe him, she thought, too tired to be angry yet. It made a good story, but she'd *heard* Liv say his name! Then, as though to prove him right, the telephone rang and he came out of the bathroom, swearing.

She had a clear view across the shadowy bedroom, into the study beyond, and she watched him take the call. 'What is it now?' he demanded as he picked up the receiver, leaning against the edge of the desk to listen, a towel in his other hand.

The desk lamp was on and angled down, casting

brilliant light on the top of the desk. Anne stared at it with a mixture of disbelief and wild optimism, noting the litter of papers, an empty glass and a coffee cup. What she had heard on the path bore no relation to what she was seeing now—and hearing too, she acknowledged when Nick spoke again.

'Look, we've beaten this subject to death,' he said impatiently. 'Show some initiative, damn it! Make the decision yourself. I don't want to hear any more!' He slammed the receiver down, waited a moment, then picked it up and stuffed it in one of the desk drawers. 'There, that's done,' he told Anne, coming back through the bedroom to where she waited for him in the doorway. 'No more calls tonight.'

It looked so good, sounded good too, but she didn't trust the evidence; she couldn't. She didn't dare. 'But you *were* with Liv,' she blurted out. 'I heard you!'

'When was that?'

'On my way back here,' she explained, afraid to meet his eyes, staring instead at his shirt front. She'd got it wet, she saw, momentarily distracted by the sight of the fine white fabric clinging damply to the powerful muscles beneath. 'I waited for hours,' she began again, forcing herself to concentrate on the issue at hand, taking refuge in indignation. 'You were gone and so was Liv. Then, coming back here, I heard Liv laughing, and she couldn't find her dress, for God's sake! *You* thought it was funny!'

'I'm sure someone did,' Nick conceded cheerfully. 'Some other poor fool.'

'But I *heard* you!'

'You only think you did,' he told her, laughing. 'It was someone else.'

'It couldn't have been,' she told him, alarmed to discover that her voice wasn't quite steady. 'She told you that you were fantastic—that you hadn't forgotten a thing, even after so long.'

'That's hardly conclusive, love. Any number of men can qualify for that particular compliment.'

'But she called you by name,' Anne objected, suddenly

close to tears. 'She called you "darling Nick"—just after you started to make love to her again.'

'No,' he contradicted flatly, draping the towel over her shoulders, his hands holding it in place. 'She was bluffing, and some poor bastard made love to her, never thinking to ask why she didn't have his name straight.

'Anne,' he continued calmly, but she could feel the strength of his grip through the towel, 'Liv must have known you were nearby, and counted on your being able to hear but not see what was going on. Love, I was here! I was in the study the whole time. I watched you undress and drop everything on the floor. I heard what you said——'

'What did I say?' she demanded, her voice muffled as he pulled the towel over her head, rubbing gently to dry her hair. 'I don't remember saying anything,' she added more clearly, standing passive before him when he moved the towel down to her shoulders again.

'The first thing you said was, "damn him". I assumed you meant me, and I decided not to interrupt until I knew *why* you were damning me. Unfortunately, you weren't too forthcoming,' he continued as she obediently held out first one arm and then the other for him to dry. 'Next, you announced—to no one in particular—that you would do as you pleased.'

'I don't remember what I said,' she told him, resting her head against his damp shirt when he began to dry her back. 'But I remember how angry I was.'

'So I gathered,' he agreed lightly, his voice close to her ear. 'Once you'd thrown yourself into the pool, you suggested that I could go to hell.'

'I remember that!' And Nick couldn't have been with Liv, she realised, not if he'd heard what she'd said. Suddenly she felt whole again, safe and contented as she leaned against him, lulled by the gentle friction of the towel against her skin. 'I was *very* angry.'

'Why, Anne?'

'It hurt—to think of you with Liv,' she explained,

incapable of anything but the truth. 'I felt betrayed, and I was jealous too.'

'Good.' In his hands, the towel was creating a deliberately sensuous effect on her senses. 'I hoped you'd tell me that.'

'Did you?' she asked vaguely, closing her eyes against a wave of giddy weakness as his arms closed around her and he carried her to the bed. 'I wonder why.'

'So do I.' She waited, suddenly alert again, knowing that he was deciding whether to end this madness between them. 'No, that's not true,' he continued, laying her down. She felt the bed shift as he leaned over her, and she slowly released the breath she had unconsciously been holding. 'I've discovered that you matter to me, that I want you,' he murmured, his lips tasting hers while the towel became an instrument of delightful torture, feathering over her breasts, her stomach, her thighs. 'It's not just friendship now. Do you understand?'

She nodded, her body beginning to stir beneath his touch.

'I want you, love,' he said again. 'I've been wanting you for days, I think, but it's no good if it's not what you want, too. That's why I hoped——' He was suddenly still, his lips withdrawn from their flickering contact with hers. 'I'll stop right now—before we go any further—if that's what you want.'

'No! That's *not* what I want,' Anne said fiercely. 'You matter. . .I want you too!'

'Good.' He got up from the bed, discarding his clothing with quick, economical movements.

Anne knew that, if she had any doubts at all, this was her last chance to stop him. But she didn't want to stop him, she knew; she wanted him, and not just for the physical pleasure she knew she would find in his arms. She loved him, and they had shared everything else in these past few weeks; it was inevitable that they share this, as well. Inevitable and very right, she decided, lifting her arms to greet him when he returned to her.

'Cool Anne,' he murmured tenderly, the rough texture of the towel replaced by the caressing warmth of his hands. 'Your skin is so cool, so soft.' His lips teased at hers while his hands learned her body: moulding the curves of her hips, spanning her waist, lingering briefly against the soft under swell of her breasts before he covered them with the warmth of his touch. 'Ah, love,' he said softly, his gaze holding hers, 'I don't know why it took so long to admit that I want you. . .need you. . .'

Her breath caught, then was released in a ragged sigh when his lips began to follow his hands. He was possessing her now, kindling her response until she was overwhelmed by sensations so sharp and sweet that her body arched towards him, desperately seeking the rest of his magic.

'Easy, love, take it slowly,' he breathed when she wrapped her arms around him, trying to draw him into the aching void he had created in her. 'Let me make it good for you.'

How much better could it be? she wondered vaguely as he continued his clever teasing, until desire dominated her being, scattering her thoughts and destroying the last vestiges of her control. Even then, through a haze of passion, she was aware of the restraint Nick was imposing on himself. There was incredible deliberation, incredible skill in the way he explored her body. He found so many new ways to please and torment her that, by the time his body finally closed over hers, she was more than ready for the final release. Her need was such a blazing fire that even the brief moment of pain was a part of the wild and piercingly sweet endless moment of consummation.

'Dear Nicholas, thank you,' she whispered with a sigh of contentment when the storm had passed and she lay, exhausted but finally complete, in his arms. 'I didn't know. . .I had no idea. . .'

'Of course not,' he murmured, kissing her gently as she settled against him and closed her eyes. 'No, you couldn't, could you?' he asked, and, tired as she was, she still heard the odd inflection in his voice. 'But I shouldn't have done this to you!'

'No, don't say that,' she told him, even as sleep began to overtake her. 'I wanted you to. . . .I didn't have any choice.'

CHAPTER NINE

ANNE awoke to the sound of rain pounding on the roof of the cottage, while in the distance, thunder rumbled indistinctly. She lay there, listening to the storm, feeling safe and protected with Nick beside her. He was turned towards her, his shoulder serving as her pillow, one of his legs sprawled across both of hers, holding her firmly to him. It was still dark, but the soft glow of the lamp in the study spilled through the open doorway and across the bed. Nick's face was hidden by shadows, but the light permitted her to see her hand when she reached out to touch his chest.

It was incredible, she mused, watching the even rise and fall of his breathing beneath her hand. She had been so tired, so utterly spent, when she had fallen asleep in his arms. Now—and it couldn't be more than a very few hours later—she was wide awake. Both her mind and her body felt unbelievably alive to him, and to all that they had shared. Finally, unable to resist, she experimentally and very gently began to explore the hard-muscled breadth of his chest.

'You'd better stop.' He sounded still half asleep, his voice an intimate and lazy murmur in the shadows. 'I'm only human, love.'

'Are you sure?' she whispered, excitement stirring within her when she felt his muscles contracting under her touch. 'Yes, I think you are,' she observed, her hand moving lower, caressing the flat planes of his stomach, listening to the sound of his sharp indrawn breath. 'You can't know what a relief it is to learn that you're not always in complete control.'

'Not possible,' he told her, his breathing already hurried and uneven, 'not when you touch me like this.'

'Good.' Her own excitement was building now, and

her hand drifted lower, smoothing over his lean hip until she encountered the frail barrier of the sheet. She tried to push it away and discovered that it was so tangled around their legs that it wouldn't move. 'The sheet's in the way,' she complained, tracing its taut edge. 'I can't go any further.'

'Get rid of it,' he urged, shifting his leg just enough to give her room to work.

She made a game of it, her fingers lingering on his skin as she worked each wrinkle free. Long before she was done, Nick's breathing had grown harsh and ragged, the sound of it encouraged her to take even greater liberties. She had, she discovered with a sense of wonder and delicious anticipation, the power to destroy his defences as thoroughly as he had destroyed hers a few hours before. She could sense the tension growing within him, feel the subtle movements of his body as he stirred restlessly against her.

'Yes. . .that's right,' he said thickly when she finally got the sheet free and pushed it away. 'Yes, love. . .don't stop.'

'I won't,' she promised just before his mouth closed hungrily over hers, and her own control began to slip. Now it was instinct which guided her hands and her lips, instinct which showed her body how to inflame his even more. How to inflame them both, she realised dimly, desire spiralling through her. Need was the imperative now, a white-hot fire which drew them together until they met as equals in that wild and abandoned moment when the fire consumed them both.

'Good lord,' Nick said at last with a deep and shuddering breath. 'How did you learn to do that?'

'You taught me, love,' she whispered, kissing him. 'I wanted to please you, this time.'

'And so you did,' he agreed lazily, pulling her even closer, so that they fell asleep in each other's arms.

When Anne awoke the next time, Nick was lying on his side, his head propped on one hand, a little distance between them as he studied her face. 'Good morning,' he said with a strange and unreadable smile. 'Did you sleep well—during those times when you slept at all?'

'Yes.' She turned her head away from his gaze as she felt her colour beginning to rise.

'No, don't. I want to be able to see you,' he told her, his fingers brushing her cheek, compelling her to turn back. 'I've been lying awake for a while, thinking.'

'Thinking what?' she asked, suddenly wary.

'About us, of course.' He smiled again, but it told her no more than the first one had. 'I'm going to marry you, Anne.'

'No!' The word was an instinctive reaction to his simple but terrifyingly final statement of fact. 'Why? because of last night?'

'Among other things.'

'No,' she said again, appalled. 'Nick, there's no need. . .you don't have to!'

'I know,' he agreed mildly, 'but it's what I *want* to do. Last night was quite remarkable, love. *You* were quite remarkable, because of what you gave me.'

'Do you mean my virginity?' she asked bitterly. 'That's no reason to feel that you've got to marry me!'

'Well, I could argue that point,' he said calmly enough, but his expression was suddenly grim. 'It was something you valued highly, and I took it without really giving you time to think.'

'You didn't take it! I *gave* it. Gladly,' she finished in a strangled voice, blushing furiously.

'And so delightfully too,' he supplied with a smile that left her feeling weak. 'That's the real point of this, love. You'll have to take my word for it, but believe me—last night was very good. So are you—and I don't just mean in bed, although that certainly helps. You're good in so many ways, about so many things. . . Good for me, I think. You're what I *should* want, and I'm convinced I can learn to love you, given time.'

'I see,' she said calmly, but her mind was working

furiously. 'What is it? Are you planning to marry me so that I can be your way to exorcise Liv?'

'Of course not.' His fingers had been resting on her cheek, but now he began to thread them slowly through her hair. 'It's not that at all, love.'

'Nick, don't,' she said weakly as he bent his head, clearly intending to kiss her. 'You confuse things when you start this. . .I can't think. . .'

'Perhaps it's better that way, love,' he murmured, his body turning to cover hers. 'Don't think. Just feel. . .just let it happen.'

Anne couldn't help herself. Her arms were already around him, drawing him closer while his lips explored her face. The madness, the magic, was starting again. . .and then they both froze as they heard the decided sound of footsteps on the veranda.

'Nick? Are you there?' called Bill, and the sound of his voice suggested that he had paused discreetly, just around the corner. 'There are problems up at the big house, and I've been sent to get you.'

Nick swore fluently under his breath, his body rigid against hers. 'For the Lord's sake, can't it wait?'

'Afraid not, big brother,' Bill answered cheerfully. 'You're needed now.'

'Then stay where you are,' Nick called impatiently. 'I'll be out in a couple of minutes. As God is my witness,' he continued to Anne, his tone savage, 'there are going to be doors on this place—and locks!' He hesitated briefly, then continued urgently, dropping his voice, 'Listen, love, we can't leave it like this. I am *not* marrying you to exorcise Liv! I am not marrying you because you were a virgin! I am marrying you because I'm *content* with you—not just satisfied, but content. What's wrong with that?'

'It's not love——'

'Of course it's love,' he interrupted to say.

'—and it's not what you feel for Liv.'

'No, it's not what I feel for Liv,' he agreed, eyes far away. 'It's very different. . . Look,' he continued, his gaze meeting hers again, 'let me get rid of Bill. Then we'll talk.' He got out of bed, took a moment to pull on a robe, then went out on to the veranda. 'All right,' he began impatiently, just out of sight, 'what's going on, that you had to barge in on us like this?'

'Damned if I know, but all hell's broken loose,' Bill explained cheerfully. 'Alex and Liv are having a blazing row. She's in a towering rage, threatening to kill him, or to take him for every penny he's got. She's even thrown in something about dragging that little nurse's name through the mud, and now the poor girl is having hysterics. The servants are keeping out of the way and enjoying the show, and Alex is having an acute anxiety attack. When I left, Liv was literally throwing things at him. When *I* tried to do something, I got a Ming vase aimed at my face.'

'What has any of that got to do with me?' Nick asked with ominous calm.

'Well, someone's got to cool things off,' said Bill, sounding vastly amused. 'I rather suspect that the fabulous invalid has done the obvious, by falling in love with his nurse, and is attempting, without much success, to boot his wife out. I really think, big brother, that you're the only one who can get things under control—*and* maybe manage to avoid a family scandal of epic proportions.'

'I see,' Nick said calmly enough, but Anne could tell that he was in a towering, but carefully controlled, rage of his own. 'All right, I'll be up as soon as I can. Did you know about this?' he demanded, appearing in the bedroom doorway just a moment later. 'You'd had suspicions, but did you *know*?'

She had had no time to prepare, no time to do anything but grab for the sheet to cover herself. Now she could only stare helplessly at him.

'Did you *know*?' he demanded again, his cold grey gaze boring through her. 'Was anything said last night, after I left?'

'I. . .' Anne swallowed nervously, knowing precisely

what he was thinking. 'Alex told me,' she admitted reluctantly, her voice a whisper.

'Is that why last night happened, Anne?' he asked with deceptive, assuredly ominous calm. 'Did you think I'd take Liv back the moment I heard that Alex didn't want her any more? Did you decide to sacrifice your virginity in some mad scheme to *save* me from her?'

'No, of course not!' she protested, but she could tell that he didn't believe her. It *looked* awful, she knew, as though she'd set about to seduce him, had trapped him into feeling he must marry her just as soon as she'd heard Liv was about to be free. 'I knew—Alex told me—but then so much else happened. . .'

'What?' Nick asked coldly.

'You were gone so long, and then I realised that Liv wasn't there either,' she explained doggedly, even though she knew it wasn't going to do any good. 'And then, when I finally left, you *know* I thought you were with her. That was *all* I was thinking about when I got back here! I'd completely forgotten what Alex had said.'

'But then, when you knew I hadn't been with her—and you *did* know that, Anne—why didn't you say something? Why didn't you *tell* me?'

'I don't know.' What *could* she tell him? she wondered wildly, staring down at her hands, studying the way they were clutching the sheet. She *couldn't* tell him she loved him! She *couldn't* explain that she'd been so caught up in how she felt about him and in what was happening between them that she'd been incapable of thinking of anything else!

She certainly hadn't been thinking about poor silly Alex and the childish mix of pride and peevishness with which he had announced his news, the way he had insisted that he be the one to tell—— 'Oh, he didn't want me to.' Thank heaven she'd remembered—and not a moment too soon, judging by Nick's expression! 'He asked me not to. He said he wanted to tell you himself.'

'Alex *asked* you——' Nick stopped abruptly, briefly pacing the room before turning back to confront her again. 'For heaven's sake, when did *Alex* begin to matter so much to you? After all that had happened between us—after all we'd been through—I can't believe that some whim of Alex's meant that much to you! Damn it, Anne, why couldn't you have been honest with me?'

Because I wasn't *thinking*! she shouted silently. I was too busy loving you—being in love with you—to think about anything else! There was the truth, but it was the last thing he'd want to hear now—now that Liv was finally free! I *can't* tell him that, Anne thought, trapped and despairing. If I tell him that, he'll pity me and feel responsible for me. . . *Pity!* No, she couldn't have that—she could stand anything but Nick's pity!—so she had to find some answer for him. 'I—you were distracting me, and——'

'Yes, I was, wasn't I?' he observed with a brief, bitter smile. 'But I gave you a chance to stop me, Anne. You could have done it—you *know* that!—but you said you wanted it too.'

'I know,' she admitted miserably.

'What is it about you?' he demanded, staring down at her, his expression suggesting that he found the whole business repulsive. 'Is it some compulsion of yours? Must you always do what you're *supposed* to?'

'What do you mean?'

'You know damn well what I mean,' he snapped, beginning to pace. 'You spent a year sacrificing yourself for Joel, and you'll go back to that the moment this is over. In the meantime, though, you did the same thing for me. Lord! You've more than earned your money, haven't you? Gone above and beyond the call of duty—and I don't know. . . Well, it raises a few difficult questions, doesn't it, Anne?'

'Yes,' she admitted tonelessly, watching as he pulled out clothes to wear and disappeared into the bathroom. She sat motionless in the middle of the bed, listening to the sound of the shower, suddenly feeling quite empty—almost dead, in fact.

'I'll be back as soon as I can,' said Nick when he came

out of the bathroom, his voice oddly weary. 'We'll settle this then.'

What was there to settle? she wondered listlessly when he'd left the cottage. He knew what she had done—at least he *thought* he knew what she had done, she corrected with careful precision, and nothing she could say would convince him that she hadn't.

She didn't see how she could face him, she thought, slowly getting out of bed, automatically taking her own shower and then dressing. He would come back from Alex and Liv, would demand more answers of her, and there was so much she couldn't explain. . . It was an impossible situation, she realised, standing alone in the centre of the empty bedroom. He would be angry with her, but he would also be pitying her, and his damned nobility would be hard at work. Was there any way, she wondered, to convince him that last night had placed him under no obligation? Could she even maintain her self-possession long enough to try? She doubted it, the way she felt right now, and she suddenly knew that she had to gain time; she had to get away from the cottage before he came back. Before she could face him calmly, she had to get her emotions under control, hide the worst of them under a careful mask.

Better still, she would *leave* now—leave and never come back, she realised as she came out of the cottage and saw Bill standing a little distance away.

'Thank goodness you're here!' she blurted out, and he grinned, tossing away a cigarette to come towards her.

'I wouldn't have missed it for the world! I heard enough to realise that two family crises have erupted this morning,' he explained cheerfully. 'I know all about the one at the big house, but I'm curious to know what's going on between you and Nick.'

'Don't you *see*?' she demanded, wondering how anyone could have missed the implications. 'Alex is going to divorce Liv, and that means Nick can have her back.'

'But Nick doesn't want her back,' Bill said easily. 'Any fool can see that he's in love with you.'

'No,' she contradicted flatly. 'It was just a game we were playing. If you think he's in love with me, it's only because he's a very good actor. And perhaps, for the last week or so, he's been a little confused about things,' she forged on, the words tumbling over each other in her imperative need to get away quickly. 'He hasn't been loving *me*; he's been loving the idea of *not* being in love with Liv. That's why I've got to leave!'

'You're not making much sense, and old Nick won't be pleased if I help you to leave,' Bill told her, his expression one of craft and calculation. 'But what the hell? I'm a sucker for a damsel in distress. Do whatever you have to do to get ready. I'll get my car.'

'Do we have time?' she asked anxiously. 'Are you sure he won't come back too soon?'

'We've got plenty of time,' he assured her with a grin. 'He's not going to untangle the mess at the big house in a hurry. We've got hours, little Anne. Don't worry!'

All she needed—all she intended—to take was her bag, with her passport and the huge sum of money Nick had given her weeks ago. But she had time, she realised, and she would use it to write him a note, to tell him the things she could tell him now—now that she knew she would never see him again. She went into his study, sat down at his littered desk, searching until she found paper and pen, then began to write.

'Nick, I'm leaving now, which is the best thing to do, and don't blame Bill for helping me. I'd have found some way to go anyway, even if he hadn't. When we made love last night, I *didn't* do it to save you from Liv! I did it because I *wanted* to—I told you so, but you aren't going to believe me. You've accused me of being Joel's puppet, but you've been almost as bad as Joel. You've always thought you knew best, knew better than *I* what I wanted or needed. You never trusted me to make the decisions that mattered—never believed that I had a will of my own. But I *do*! I wanted what happened last night. If I hadn't, I would have told you so. I'm leaving today, and that's my decision too. This way, you won't have to feel *responsible* for me any more. I'm sick to death of your always having to feel responsible for me! Even if you'd come back from untangling things between Alex and Liv and still wanted to marry me, I would have said no. I couldn't accept the kind of marriage you offered. It wasn't enough. You've got Liv now, or you will as soon as her divorce is final, but I still think you're a fool. What's bizarre is that, in spite of everything, you still managed to teach me what I couldn't manage to teach you. I love you, Nicholas Thayer—and I wouldn't have dared say *that* if I didn't have a will of my own!'

There! she thought defiantly, let him make what he pleased of all that! She folded the sheet of paper, leaned it against the desk lamp, then picked up her bag and prepared to leave.

As she went along the veranda, she paused in the bedroom doorway, overcome briefly by a wave of longing as she remembered last night. It had all ended so soon—*too* soon, she told herself, and for a moment the pain was more than she could bear. Then she squared her shoulders and turned away, telling herself that she mustn't ever think of last night. It had been very wrong—*not* because she and Nick had made love, but because she hadn't stopped to consider all the problems those few stolen hours would create.

'I never thought to ask,' she said to Bill as she came down the steps and found him seated behind the wheel of his bright red sports car. 'Where will you take me?'

'To the airfield. There's a plane leaving in an hour or so. I checked, and they'll hold a place for you.' He eyed her curiously as she got in beside him. 'Aren't you taking anything with you?'

'No. Well, a great deal of cash Nick gave me. I'll need it, just at first, until I find a job. Everything else was his—things he gave me—so I left them behind.' She'd *had* to leave everything, she thought with a pang—the clothes, the jewellery, especially the lease and the bankbook. To take anything implied that this had been a job, and she refused to remember it that way. 'I can pay him the money back. I will—you can tell him that if he mentions it.'

'He's not going to mention the money,' Bill told her with obvious relish. 'He's going to be absolutely furious that you've gone, and the money will be the least of it. Lord, I can't *wait* to see his face!'

'You sound like you plan to enjoy it!'

'Oh, I will, little Anne,' he agreed cheerfully. 'You can't imagine what fun it will be to have had a hand in crossing old Nick!'

'You're as bad as Alex! What *is* it about this family?' Anne asked, staring at him in perplexity. 'Doesn't anyone give a damn about anyone else?'

'You've got it,' he admitted unrepentantly. 'We weren't taught anything different, and crossing each other is one of our favourite indoor sports. The only trouble is that it's damn hard to do to old Nick—he's too self-sufficient. Alex was lucky to be given such a beautiful opportunity, and he kept it going for years. I haven't had much success, but getting you off the island—and out of Nick's life—is better than nothing. If I thought it would work, I'd pull the same stunt Alex did with Liv, but I have the feeling that nothing could get you to stick with me.'

'You're right,' Anne said shortly, grateful when Bill took the hint and didn't talk any more on the short trip to the landing field.

'I'm not going to stay with you,' he told her as he dropped her at the door of the small building which served as a terminal. 'I'd rather not be around if Nick happens to track you down before your plane leaves.'

'Is that likely to happen?'

'Of course not! It's just that I like to play things safe. I *told* you, little Anne, he'll be tied up at the big house for hours yet. Have a good trip.' Before she could get out of the car, he had leaned over and planted a kiss full on her mouth. 'Too bad there wasn't time to get something going with you—I'd have liked that. Still, maybe I'll see you again some time. Are you going back to New York?'

'I haven't decided,' Anne said coldly, getting out of the car and slamming the door, marching into the terminal building without a backward glance.

She bought a ticket to Martinique, then sat down to endure the nightmare of waiting until she could get on the plane and leave the island behind. Bill's comment about Nick tracking her down had come back to haunt her, and she was terrified each time she heard a car or someone walked into the building. She realised now that she had burned her bridges with a vengeance when she'd written the note. After the things she'd said in it, she *couldn't* face Nick again! The minutes crawled by until it was time for the little plane to leave, until she and the five other passengers who had arrived to wait with her were told that they could board.

With the others, she went out into the heat of the midday sun, reflected up from the tarmac with palpable force. She had already started towards the plane when she heard a jeep charge into the parking area and stop right beside the terminal building. There was no need to wonder; even before Nick called her name, she knew he'd come. She looked despairingly at the plane, only some fifty feet away, then braced herself as she heard Nick's footsteps pounding towards her.

'Damn it, Anne!' He reached her, grabbing her arm with one hand, the other holding the note she'd left on his desk. 'Did you mean this?' he demanded, thrusting the note at her. 'Did you mean what you said?'

She'd put herself on the line when she'd written that note; now she could either try to lie her way out of the things she'd said or find the courage to be honest. She took a deep breath, staring defiantly at him until she finally said, 'Yes.'

'Are you sure, Anne?'

'*Yes*, damn you!'

'Well——' Her answer, or the force of it, seemed to have stopped him in his tracks. He stood motionless, still gripping her arm, a towering, powerful figure in the same jeans and knit shirt he had been wearing when he had left her. 'In that case,' he began, back in stride again—in control, she thought resentfully, 'you're coming with me.'

'No! You can't just order me around any more,' she told him, refusing to budge when he tried to force her. 'I won't have it, Nick!'

'Then I'll *ask*,' he snapped, dropping her arm as though it had burned him. '*Will* you come with me?'

'Why?'

'So that we can straighten this out.'

'There you go!' she exploded, so angry that she was shaking. 'Being *responsible* again!'

'It's not that,' he said cautiously, almost warily, she thought. 'I just want a chance to explain things to you.'

'No, Nick.' She shook her head, ignoring the circle of curious faces around them. 'Explaining won't do any good. I already understand—it's all part of the same thing, the same *problem*. You don't need to explain what I already know!'

'I see.' His face looked pale beneath the tan. 'Is that your last word?'

'Yes.' The word hung between them while they stared at each other for what seemed to Anne like ages.

'Anne,' Nick began quickly, then paused. 'Is there anything else I can say? Anything that will make you stay?'

'No, Nick.' She hadn't known how much it would hurt, how much pain it would cause. She turned quickly away, so that he wouldn't be able to see her face, then started slowly towards the plane.

'Damn it, Anne!' She had only taken a few steps when

he called to her, his tone fierce and urgent—and oddly anguished. 'I *love* you!'

'Oh. . . Well. . .' She stopped, turned again, turned back to him this time. 'In *that* case,' she said with a brilliant smile, oblivious to the tears on her face. 'In that case, I'll stay!'

'Thank God!' He closed the distance between them, put his arms very gently around her, staring down at her, devouring her with his eyes. 'We've got so much talking to do.'

'You're not just being noble again, are you?' she asked, more frightened than she was willing to admit to herself.

'No, love.' He smiled for the first time. 'I'm not being noble—believe me.' He reached up with one hand to wipe the tears from her face. 'I'm being selfish. I can't help myself.'

'Well, it's about time.' Anne nodded approvingly. 'I was afraid you'd never do it.'

'Do what?'

'Be selfish. Let someone help you.' Her spirits soaring, she threw her arms around him. 'Stop doing *everything* yourself!'

'Is that what I've been doing?' he asked, sounding startled.

'Oh, yes, love—all your life, I think.'

'And you're about to change all that?'

'Of course,' she answered quickly, then hesitated, suddenly shy. '*If* you'll let me.'

'I doubt that I'll have a choice,' he told her drily. 'After all, as you said in your note, you have a will of your own.'

'And I intend to use it,' she promised, standing on tiptoe to kiss him.

'But in private from now on,' he said, a little unsteadily, when she was done. 'I think we'd better leave, love—before we disgrace ourselves in public.'

'The cottage doesn't have any doors,' she reminded him.

'I know,' he grinned, turning her towards the jeep, his arm still around her. 'I've found a way to handle that.'

'Nick?' Later—much later—feeling more contented, more complete, than she ever had before, Anne stirred lazily in the circle of his arms. 'Will Kitt and Winnie trade houses with us?'

'Why?' he asked absently, his lips against her temple.

'Because I like it here.' In fact, she had loved it on sight—the little pastel building, hardly more than a shack on stilts, tucked in among the flowering shrubs, at the edge of the beach just beyond the headland where Nick's cottage stood. On the lower level, there was one big room, combining living, dining and kitchen space. Above, up a winding flight of stairs, was a sleeping loft, very simple, just plain white walls, a bureau, a blanket chest, and the double bed where she lay in Nick's arms. And the three wide windows with their views of the sea, she remembered, her eyes drawn to the glorious colour as the setting sun stained the water.

When Nick had led her up to the sleeping loft in the early afternoon, wooden shutters had been closed across the windows, permitting entry only to the cool breeze and the scent of flowers. There, in shadowy darkness and splendid isolation, they had made love in the truest sense of the words—with fire, passion, tenderness and wild intensity. Finally satisfied and complete, they had slept, then awakened to come together again with even more feeling and a heightened awareness of the magic between them. At last, in the hushed hour before sunset, Nick had got up long enough to open the shutters, and now they lay together, bathed in a fiery glow.

'I could stay here forever,' Anne told him, and saw his slow smile.

'Not possible, I'm afraid,' he said, sounding still half asleep, or perhaps just at peace with himself. 'We'll have to leave some time.'

'Why?' she asked, making a face at him. 'Because you're hungry, I suppose.'

'Because—no,' he checked himself. 'Last time I *told* you, and that didn't work. This time I'll *ask*. Anne, my love, will you marry me? Some time soon? Whenever we can bring ourselves to leave here?'

'I suppose so,' she agreed, pretending reluctance. 'It won't be easy, but some time. . .if you'll have me.'

'If I'll have you? Is there any doubt? Ah, my love, I can't live without you.' Nick sighed, drawing her even closer, cradling her against him, his head bent close to hers. 'I don't have a choice.'

'No?'

'None,' he answered simply. 'You're my life now. I think I've been falling in love with you from the start— since that first night in Joel's loft when I was charmed by the daughter of two ageing flower children, by a girl who wore an absurd Edwardian wedding dress and had the most amazingly conventional ideas about marriage.

'None of which included me,' he continued after a moment, a reminiscent smile playing at the corners of his mouth. 'From the beginning, I was furious with you for caring so much about Joel, but I never stopped to wonder *why* it bothered me so.'

'You were trying to open my eyes,' she suggested lightly. 'Saving me from myself.'

'No. It was that I'd never seen such clarity of purpose before, such loyalty—to someone who didn't deserve it. You had so much warmth, so much love to give, and I knew it was all being wasted on the wrong man. I think I was already jealous, that I wanted—even needed—you for myself, but I wasn't ready to admit it to myself. I was too busy playing the fool, and it went on so long. Do you remember that other time I suggested that we ought to get married?'

'Vividly,' she agreed, her tone so dry that he winced. 'I wanted to slap you.'

'You should have. It might have knocked some sense into me.'

'I doubt it,' she told him with a brief smile. 'You were

too busy trying to save me from Joel *and* yourself from Liv. You weren't ready to be sensible yet.'

'You call this sensible?' Nick asked with ironic amusement, his fingers toying briefly with her hair before beginning to trace the delicate curve of her cheek. 'Funny, but sensible isn't the word I'd choose.'

'I suppose you're right.' Anne stretched luxuriously as his hand came to rest on her shoulder. 'Sensible doesn't make it. How about real—is that better? That day you told me we should consider getting married, you still weren't being real.'

'But I was,' he corrected, his hand moving slowly across her shoulder and down her arm in a warm caress. 'That decision was about as real as I'd ever been in my life. I'd found what I wanted—and needed—in you. Already, the idea of going on without you was unthinkable, so I had to find some way to keep you with me. I knew what I wanted by then; it's just that I still couldn't admit it to myself or to you. So I came up with that insane business proposal. It was the best I could do at the time, the only thing I knew how to do. Even this morning, I was still talking about how I could learn to love you—as though it hadn't already happened. The trouble was that I knew nothing *about* love. There hadn't been any to speak of in my life, and I didn't know what it was when it hit me.

'So I went on wanting Liv,' he continued, his eyes briefly clouded with pain, 'and it took me what seems like forever to understand that I didn't want her at all, to see what she really was. I think, if I'd seen her at all during the last three years, I'd have seen through her sooner or later. The trouble was that I didn't. She was always this remote, unobtainable figure, and I was so fixed on wanting what I didn't have. . .'

'Just as *I* was fixed on Joel, because he wouldn't give me what I wanted.' Anne pulled a little away from Nick, straightening up as she reacted to this new knowledge. 'He wouldn't listen to me or care about me; he only took things from me and cared about what I could do for him.

Don't you see? Even though I lived with him and saw him every day, he was just as unobtainable as Liv was to you! We were both chasing after what we couldn't have, thinking that was what we wanted.'

'We were both being incredible fools, love,' Nick corrected on a teasing note, 'both making fools of ourselves and each other. All those weeks of fighting each other, of not giving in to what had already happened between us.'

'Except for last night,' she offered shyly. 'Last night we weren't fighting each other, and it was—rather grand.'

'Only "rather grand"?' he asked sceptically. 'I'd say it went far beyond that! I'd say it was heaven, sheer bliss, the most incredible, beautiful thing. . . Until this morning,' he resumed after a moment, serious now, even grim. 'Then, when Bill told me about Alex and I found out that he'd told you last night, I was so afraid that you'd done it again.'

'Done what again?' Anne asked in confusion.

'Been compelled to sacrifice yourself for someone else. You'd already done it for Joel, when you went into this mad scheme with me, and I was afraid that I was nothing more than your latest cause. I'd wanted your love, and it suddenly seemed that all I'd had was the results of this compulsion you seem to have to *save* people.'

'But I hadn't been trying to save you,' she said gravely. 'I couldn't help myself—didn't *want* to. I'd been wanting you for so long, caring about you, needing to feel complete. Needing you, love.' She leaned slightly forward, touching her fingers to first his cheek, then his lips. 'By last night, I could finally admit that you were everything to me. You still are, and you always will be. . .I *love* you, Nicholas Thayer!'

'So you said in your note,' he agreed, his voice thickening slightly as he watched her bend towards him, her hair falling around his face as her lips replaced her fingers to tease at the corners of his mouth.

'Oh, Nick,' she said, sounding shaken. 'I—are Kitt

and Winnie going to want their bed back tonight?' she asked, straightening up again, creating a little distance between them.

'No, love. When Kitt came up to the big house to let me know that he'd seen you leave with Bill, I told him that I'd bring you back, and *he* said that we'd need a private place. This is ours, for as long as we please.'

'So there's time for me to make love to you?' she asked unevenly.

'All the time in the world,' he assured her, waiting, watching her closely. '*If* that's what you want?'

'Oh, it is,' she whispered, bending to him again. 'For the rest of our lives—*if* you'll have me?'

'I'll have you,' Nick promised roughly as his arms came around her, the strength of his feelings and his embrace leaving no room for doubt in his mind or hers.

Take 4 bestselling love stories FREE

Plus get a FREE surprise gift!

HARLEQUIN'S "BIG WIN"
SWEEPSTAKES RULES & REGULATIONS
NO PURCHASE NECESSARY TO ENTER OR RECEIVE A PRIZE

1. To enter and join the Reader Service, scratch off the metallic strips on all your BIG WIN tickets #1-#6. This will reveal the values for each sweepstakes entry number, the number of free book(s) you will receive and your free bonus gift as part of our Reader Service. If you do not wish to take advantage of our Reader Service but wish to enter the Sweepstakes only, scratch off the metallic strips on your BIG WIN tickets #1-#4. Return your entire sheet of tickets intact. Incomplete and/or inaccurate entries are ineligible for that section or sections of prizes. Not responsible for mutilated or unreadable entries or inadvertent printing errors. Mechanically reproduced entries are null and void.

2. Whether you take advantage of this offer or not, your Sweepstakes numbers will be compared against the list of winning numbers generated at random by the computer. In the event that all prizes are not claimed by March 31, 1992, a random drawing will be held from all qualified entries received from March 30, 1990 to March 31, 1992, to award all unclaimed prizes. All cash prizes (Grand to Sixth), will be mailed to the winners and are payable by check in U.S. funds. Seventh prize will be shipped to winners via third-class mail. These prizes are in addition to any free, surprise or mystery gifts that might be offered. Versions of this sweepstakes with different prizes of approximate equal value may appear at retail outlets or in other mailings by Torstar Corp. and its affiliates.

3. The following prizes are awarded in this sweepstakes: ★ Grand Prize (1) $1,000,000; First Prize (1) $25,000; Second Prize (1) $10,000; Third Prize (5) $5,000; Fourth Prize (10) $1,000; Fifth Prize (100) $250; Sixth Prize (2,500) $10; ★ ★ Seventh Prize (6,000) $12.95 ARV.

   ★ This presentation offers a Grand Prize of a $1,000,000 annuity. Winner will receive $33,333.33 a year for 30 years without interest totalling $1,000,000.

   ★ ★ Seventh Prize: A fully illustrated hardcover book published by Torstar Corp. Approximate retail value of the book is $12.95.

   Entrants may cancel the Reader Service at anytime without cost or obligation to buy (see details in center insert card).

4. This Sweepstakes is being conducted under the supervision of an independent judging organization. By entering this Sweepstakes, each entrant accepts and agrees to be bound by these rules and the decisions of the judges, which shall be final and binding. Odds of winning in the random drawing are dependent upon the total number of entries received. Taxes, if any, are the sole responsibility of the winners. Prizes are nontransferable. All entries must be received at the address printed on the reply card and must be postmarked no later than 12:00 MIDNIGHT on March 31, 1992. The drawing for all unclaimed sweepstakes prizes will take place May 30, 1992, at 12:00 NOON, at the offices of Marden-Kane, Inc., Lake Success, New York.

5. This offer is open to residents of the U.S., the United Kingdom, France and Canada, 18 years or older, except employees and their immediate family members of Torstar Corp., its affiliates, subsidiaries, and all other agencies and persons connected with the use, marketing or conduct of this sweepstakes. All Federal, State, Provincial and local laws apply. Void wherever prohibited or restricted by law. Any litigation within the Province of Quebec respecting the conduct and awarding of a prize in this publicity contest must be submitted to the Régie des loteries et courses du Québec.

6. Winners will be notified by mail and may be required to execute an affidavit of eligibility and release, which must be returned within 14 days after notification or an alternative winner will be selected. Canadian winners will be required to correctly answer an arithmetical skill-testing question administered by mail, which must be returned within a limited time. Winners consent to the use of their names, photographs and/or likenesses for advertising and publicity in conjunction with this and similar promotions without additional compensation. For a list of major winners, send a stamped, self-addressed envelope to: WINNERS LIST, c/o Harlequin Reader Service, 3010 Walden Ave., P.O. Box 1396, Buffalo, NY 14269-1396. Winners Lists will be fulfilled after the May 30, 1992 drawing date.

If Sweepstakes entry form is missing, please print your name and address on a 3″ ×5″ piece of plain paper and send to:

In the U.S.
Harlequin's "BIG WIN" Sweepstakes
3010 Walden Ave.
P.O. Box 1867
Buffalo, NY 14269-1867

In Canada
Harlequin's "BIG WIN" Sweepstakes
P.O. Box 609
Fort Erie, Ontario
L2A 5X3

Offer limited to one per household.

LTY-H191R